CHARMING A KNIGHT IN COWBOY BOOTS

Copyright © 2022 by Katie Lane

All rights reserved. Except for use in any review, the reproduction or utilization of this work in whole or in part in any form by any electronic, mechanical or other means, now known or hereinafter invented, including xerography, photocopying and recording, or in any information storage or retrieval system, is forbidden without the written permission of the publisher.

This book is a work of fiction. Names, characters, places, and incidents are a product of the writer's imagination. All rights reserved. Scanning, uploading, and electronic sharing of this book without the permission of the author is unlawful piracy and theft. To obtain permission to excerpt portions of the text, please contact the author at katie@katielanebooks.com Thank you for respecting this author's hard work and livelihood.

Printed in the USA.

Cover Design and Interior Format
© THE KILLION GROUP INC

# Charming a KNIGHT in COWBOY BOOTS

Kingman Ranch
· 2 ·

# KATIE LANE

*To Christy Ann, my beloved sister
and biggest cheerleader*

# CHAPTER ONE

BE CAREFUL WHAT you wish for.
Adeline Raquel Kingman hadn't followed this golden rule, and subsequently, she was destined to live her life regretting it. Wishes held power. More power than she had ever imagined. Once she'd realized that, it was too late. Her wishes had already been granted . . . in the worst possible ways. Now she was careful not to wish for anything. She didn't blow out birthday candles, break wishbones, care if the clock read 11:11, carefully pick up fallen eyelashes, notice rainbows . . . or toss coins into fountains.

She looked down at the coins that littered the bottom of the fountain her grandfather, "King" Kingman, had shipped across the Atlantic for his garden. Beneath the moonlit water, the pennies, nickels, dimes, and quarters glittered like sunken treasure. Like sunken treasure, some coins were cursed. Or at least, Adeline's were. If she knew which coins were hers, she'd jump into the fountain and reclaim her wishes.

But it wouldn't turn back time.

It wouldn't bring back her mother and father.

Or Danny, the boy she had loved for most of her life.

A wave of tiredness washed over her. She was used to the feeling. She hadn't slept well in months and usually felt exhausted and drained. It took a real effort to get through each day. But she did. Not for herself, but for her three brothers and sister. If it were up to Adeline, she would continue to hide away in her tower room. But she couldn't do that to Stetson, Wolfe, Delaney, and Buck. They had been through enough without having to worry about her.

Still, it was exhausting to pretend everything was all right when everything felt all wrong. It had taken all her energy to smile and greet guests at Stetson's wedding reception. Which was why she had escaped and was hiding in the hedge labyrinth. She'd thought if she just had a few minutes alone to collect herself, she would be able to continue the farce. But now she felt even more drained. Like a flower deprived of water and sunlight.

She lay back on the cold stone ledge that ran along the fountain, resting her arm in the cast across her stomach. If she could just take a short catnap, maybe she would have enough energy to make it through the rest of the reception. Just five minutes of sleep was all she needed. Just five short minutes of oblivion with no memories or guilt.

Was that too much to ask?

She closed her eyes. But just as the fog of oblivion descended, she was pulled back to harsh reality.

"Miss Kingman."

She opened her eyes and turned her head. She could just make out the shape of a cowboy in the shadows. His broad shoulders filled the opening between the hedges, and the crown of his hat almost reached the top of the high, neatly trimmed shrubs.

There was only one ranch hand that big.

She quickly got up and tried to act like sleeping on a fountain ledge during a wedding reception was a completely normal thing to do. "Yes, Mr. Reardon? What did you need?"

Gage Reardon's large, shadowy form didn't move. Or speak. He rarely spoke to her. He always directed his comments or replies to her brother, Stetson. Stetson found it amusing that Adeline's beauty left Gage flustered. She didn't agree. Gage wasn't the type of man who got flustered. He just didn't think she was worthy of his attention.

Which annoyed her.

"Did you hear me, Mr. Reardon?" she asked. "Or do you need my brother here to translate?"

She could feel his hard gaze, and it was a struggle not to fidget beneath it. Finally, after what felt like forever, he spoke. "You shouldn't be out here all by yourself, Miss Kingman. You need to get back to the party."

She knew he was just following orders. Stetson's orders. Ever since the accident, Adeline had not been allowed to do anything alone. If her three brothers weren't keeping watch over her, this man was. And she was sick of it. She wasn't a sheep who needed a shepherd.

She stood and shook the wrinkles out of her lavender maid of honor gown. "I realize you're Stetson's right hand man. But you don't give me orders, Mr. Reardon. I'll go back to the reception when I want to go back to the reception." She waited for him to leave.

Unfortunately, he didn't. He just continued to stand there as still as the bronze horse statues placed throughout the garden.

She crossed her arms to show her annoyance—which was difficult with her cast. "Is there something else you needed?"

"No, ma'am."

"Then why are you still here?"

There was another long pause. "Because you are."

She dropped her arms. "So you aren't going to leave until I do?"

"Pretty much."

Now thoroughly ticked, she took a few steps closer. "I'm ordering you to leave."

"I don't take my orders from you, Miss Kingman. I take them from your brother. And he's asked me to keep an eye on his family. You included. I won't have something happening to you on my watch." His cowboy hat dipped, and she knew he looked at her cast. "You should understand that after what happened to you and Stetson."

She huffed out her breath. "Believe me, I do understand, but I seriously doubt that whoever tampered with the brakes on Stetson's truck and caused our accident is stupid enough to try something in the middle of a wedding reception attended by the entire town."

"What makes you think that would be stupid?"

"Because he'd be caught. All I have to do is scream and my brothers—"

For a large man, Gage moved quickly. Before Adeline realized what was happening, he had a hand over her mouth and she was pinned against his rock-solid body.

Adeline suddenly felt like she had been plugged into a power source. A sizzling current raced through her, obliterating her exhaustion. After months of feeling absolutely nothing, she *felt*. She felt her heart thumping madly beneath her rib cage. Blood racing through her veins. Her lungs expanding with every breath. And her nerves tingling on every square inch of her skin.

She was terrified.

Not of Gage. She knew he was just trying to prove a point. She was terrified of all the feelings that seemed to be gushing up from the vault she'd locked them in. She hadn't felt like this since before Danny died—or possibly even before that. And she didn't want to feel. It was much better not to. But when Gage spoke close to her ear, his deep voice caused every cell in her body to awaken and feel alive.

"Right now, Miss Kingman, I could do whatever I wanted to you and there's nothing you could do to stop me." He tightened his arm around her waist. Not painfully, just enough to demonstrate his strength.

She didn't need the lesson. She was already extremely aware of the muscles that surrounded her. And everything else about Gage Reardon. The warmth of his breath against her ear. The rise and fall of his chest against her back. The bulge of his bicep against her breast. The warm skin of his hand against her mouth.

He shifted that hand and his calloused palm brushed her lips. A flash of heat spiked through her. Heat that she'd never felt before. Not even with Danny. Terror turned to panic. She needed to get away from this man. She needed to get away now.

When his grip on her mouth loosened, she bit down hard on his finger. He released her with a muffled oath just as her brother called out her name.

"Addie! Addie!" Wolfe came running through the opening in the hedge. He stopped short when he saw them and heaved a relieved breath. "There you are. I thought you'd left the reception alone. I didn't know you were with Gage."

All Adeline had to do was tell her brother what Gage had done, and he'd be fired on the spot. And probably beaten to a pulp as well. Her brothers respected Gage and valued his dedication and loyalty to the family, but they were extremely protective of her and her sister, Delaney. If Adeline told them that Gage had gotten out of line, he'd be gone from the Kingman Ranch by morning. Adeline couldn't say she would be sorry to see him go. She didn't know what had just happened, but she didn't want it to happen again.

And yet, she couldn't bring herself to say anything.

At least, not yet.

Not when someone was out to get her family and had mutilated and killed one of their bulls; set their barn on fire; assaulted a stable hand and her new sister-in-law, Lily; and tampered with the brakes on Stetson's truck, almost killing him and Adeline. Whoever it was had gotten more and more daring, and next time someone could actually die.

The thought frightened Adeline. She couldn't lose anyone else. While she might not like the way Gage had manhandled her tonight, she knew he'd only done it to make her understand the danger she'd put herself in. Stetson trusted Gage to watch out for the family. That's exactly what Gage had been doing. His methods might've been extreme, but he hadn't actually hurt her. Now that he wasn't touching her, the feelings he'd evoked had receded back into their vault.

"As you can see, I'm fine, Wolfe," she said. "You don't have to be worried about me."

Gage ratted her out. "Yes, you do. Your sister came out here alone. Something you would've known if you'd been doing your job of watching out for her—instead of chasing after all the single women at the reception."

She waited for Wolfe to set him straight. Her little brother was a charmer with women, but he could have a bad temper with men. Especially if they challenged him. But instead of bristling at Gage's reprimand, Wolfe laughed.

"Do you ever take a break, Gage? Okay, so I fell down on my job. You should try it some time. I heard that Wally Rondo's daughter is interested in you. You can't tell me you wouldn't like to spend some time alone with that cute little farmer's daughter."

"I'm working tonight."

"You're always working. You and my brother are two peas in a pod." Wolfe grinned. "But even Stetson stopped working long enough to find himself a woman. Go ask Miley Rondo to dance, Gage. You've certainly earned some time off. I won't tell Stetson and I'll take over keeping an eye on Adeline."

"I don't dance," Gage said.

Wolfe shrugged. "Suit yourself. But if you don't want to have fun, you shouldn't mind if I have some."

"It's not my job to have—" Before Gage could finish, Wolfe disappeared through the opening in the hedge.

Since Adeline wanted to be stuck with Gage as much as he wanted to be stuck with her, she quickly followed her brother. As a kid, she had played often in the labyrinth so she had no trouble finding her way out. Gage didn't make a sound, but she knew he followed close behind her. As she started to climb the stone steps that led to the garden where the reception was being held, he stopped her.

"Please don't leave the reception alone again."

It was still an order, but at least this time he'd said please. She turned and found him standing at the bottom of the steps. He looked up at her, and the lights strung throughout the garden fell across his face. He wasn't what she would call a handsome man. His features were all harsh angles: Square chin with a cleft. Pronounced jaw that was always covered in golden stubble. Wide mouth that rarely smiled—at least not at her. A nose that sat at an odd angle as if it had been broken and not properly set. Sharp cheekbones. Deep-set eyes. Broad forehead.

His only soft features were his eyes. They were hazel—more gold than green—and surrounded by long, lush lashes that any woman would envy. They stared back at her, waiting for some kind of confirmation.

"I won't leave the reception," she said.

He studied her for a long moment before he nodded. "Then goodnight, Miss Kingman."

He turned and disappeared into the darkness.

Leaving her alone once again.

# Chapter Two

THE WEDDING RECEPTION ended around midnight.

After all the guests had gone home and the caterers had cleaned up, Gage checked to make sure the horse stables were secure before he headed to the bunkhouse. He used the bathroom and brushed his teeth, then headed back out the door with his sleeping bag.

The repairs to the barn roof had been completed, but the scaffolding remained—on his orders. Gage climbed to the top platform and rolled out his sleeping bag before taking off his hat and tugging off his boots. Both socks had holes in them. As did most of his other socks. And a few pairs of his boxer shorts. He really needed to get into town and buy himself some new underwear and socks, and maybe a couple more t-shirts. But with all that had been happening on the ranch, he just hadn't had time.

He picked up the night vision binoculars he kept rolled in his sleeping bag and scanned as much of the ranch as he could see. The pastures, the paddocks, the stable grounds, the gardens, the lake . . . and finally the Kingmans' house.

A year ago, if someone had told him there were castles in Texas, he would have thought they were delusional. It wasn't until he arrived at the Kingman Ranch that he discovered the truth. The three-story monstrosity the Kingmans called home looked just like a castle with its tall stone turrets, ornate windows, and thick oak doors.

The castle even had a princess.

He shifted his binoculars to the only light on in the castle, shining like a lighthouse from the top of one tower. Through the glass of the balcony doors, he could clearly see the Kingman princess. She had hair as long and golden as Rapunzel's. A complexion as creamy as Snow White's. Eyes as blue as Cinderella's.

And a personality as icy as the princess from *Frozen* whose name he could never remember.

He had no trouble remembering Adeline Kingman's name. The first time he'd seen a picture of her, he'd been struck speechless by her beauty. But beauty was only skin deep. He'd learned that beneath the perfect features was a spoiled, arrogant woman. A woman who could work her wiles on a man, then completely rip his heart out.

Gage had come to Kingman Ranch wanting revenge for the damage Adeline Kingman had done. He still did. But to take revenge on Adeline would also mean taking revenge on Stetson. In the last year, Stetson had become like a brother to Gage. He was a good man who had suffered enough grief in his life. He'd lost his mother and father and had to take on the responsibility of caring for his siblings and running a huge ranching business at an early age. As much as Gage was dying to get revenge for what Adeline had done, he couldn't do it at Stetson's expense. He couldn't even tell him the truth about his sister.

Adeline wasn't suffering from a broken heart.

She was suffering from guilt.

He focused his attention back to the window. Adeline had moved out to the balcony and was leaning on the railing like a princess waiting for her prince to scale the tower walls. He wondered if she was thinking about Danny. Or was she thinking about what had happened in the garden that very night?

Gage shouldn't have grabbed her.

Stetson had stressed one rule when Gage came to work on the ranch: stay away from his sisters. But Adeline's selfishness had sent him over the edge. He'd wasted a good thirty minutes trying to track her down after she disappeared from the wedding reception and what had she been doing? Napping! She hadn't cared that she'd taken Gage from his duties of making sure the rest of the guests were safe. All she'd cared about were her own selfish needs. If she was tired, she should get her ass to bed earlier instead of staying up half the night wandering her room and the balcony like a ghost.

Of course, he should talk. He was exhausted, but he avoided sleep too. In sleep, his mind wandered to places he didn't ever want to go back to. To desert heat and cold fear. To running from death and becoming death. Even sitting on hard scaffolding peering in a castle window at a frozen princess he hated was preferable to the terror of sleep.

But eventually sleep always caught up with him.

When the ice princess finally went back inside and turned off the lights, Gage lowered the binoculars and stretched out on his sleeping bag. The sky held about a zillion stars. Was there a heaven among those stars? Some celestial place where all good souls went after they died? If there was, he hoped as soon as you walked through the pearly gates, all your bad memories were erased. He wished that for Danny. For all his Marine buddies who had died. And for himself.

But with all the lives Gage had taken, he doubted he'd get to see heaven.

He closed his eyes and let sleep finally pull him under.

He woke to the soft pink of a dawn sky . . . and the earth trembling beneath him. For a second, he thought that Cursed, Texas, could add earthquakes to its list of catastrophes. The small town had gotten its name after being plagued with tornadoes, droughts, floods, heat waves, and almost every other calamity known to man. An earthquake wouldn't come as a surprise. But then Gage realized the earth wasn't shaking. The scaffolding was.

He rolled onto his stomach and looked over the edge. Stetson stood at the bottom. He didn't look happy. Obviously, the princess had told big brother what had happened in the garden and Gage was about to get his ass fired. He was surprised by how depressed that made him. Especially when he had never intended to stay at the Kingman Ranch for long. But working the horse ranch had given him purpose. While the nightmares of Iraq still plagued his sleep, they no longer plagued his waking hours. He didn't want to give up his daytime peace.

But it looked like he didn't have a choice.

"Mornin', Boss," he called to Stetson. "I'll be right down." He tugged on his boots and pulled on his hat, then rolled the binoculars into his sleeping bag before climbing down. Once he was on the ground, he braced for a punch. Instead, Stetson sighed and shook his head.

"It seems that Wolfe stopped by Nasty Jack's last night after the reception and got into a bar fight. He's cooling his heels in the county jail as we speak."

Gage's shoulders relaxed. Surprisingly, the princess hadn't said anything. No doubt because she didn't want Stetson to get mad at her for leaving the reception. "Sorry, Boss," Gage said. "You want me to go bail him out?"

"No. Let him stay there for another night. He needs to learn that I'm not going to bail him out every time he gets in trouble. But his shenanigans last night have made me realize that I can't trust Wolfe to take over while I'm on my honeymoon."

Gage had to agree. He hadn't been keen on Wolfe taking over the ranch from the get-go. Wolfe was a nice guy and Gage liked him, but there was a restlessness about him that made him unpredictable. He could be charming one second and volatile the next.

"So who are you thinking about putting in charge?" Gage asked. "Buck or Delaney? I'm thinking Delaney. Buck is a little too immature and irresponsible."

"Delaney is a hard worker, but she thinks too much with her heart. If I leave her in charge, the ranch will become a refuge for every misfit and abused animal in the state."

That only left one Kingman. The princess. If Stetson left his selfish oldest sister in charge, there might not be a ranch to come back to. "Are you sure, Boss?" he asked. "I mean, Adeline doesn't seem to know a lot about ranching."

Stetson grinned. "Actually, you'd be surprised how much she knows." Gage seriously doubted it. "But I'm not going to leave Adeline in charge either. She's still too upset about Danny to take on the burden of the ranch." Gage struggled to keep from letting out a contentious snort. "There's only one person I trust to do the job," Stetson continued. "That's you."

Gage was more than a little stunned. He knew Stetson trusted him to get any job done, but he had never thought he'd want him to take over the family business while he was gone. Especially when he had so many siblings. Gage felt honored and flattered.

Stetson took his silence for something else. "I know it's a lot to ask, Gage. Especially with everything going on." He sighed. "Maybe I should just cancel my trip."

"You can't cancel your trip," Gage said. "Ticking off your wife is no way to start a marriage. I'll be happy to take over while you're gone." He paused. "But are you sure your siblings are going to be okay with this?" He knew of one princess who wouldn't be. Adeline had made it clear last night that she didn't like to be ordered around by the hired help. He doubted she liked to be ordered around by anyone.

"It doesn't matter if they're okay with it. They own shares of the business, but I'm the one in charge. And if I say you're taking over while I'm gone, they'll just have to live with it." He thumped Gage on the arm. "Thank you. I can leave knowing the ranch is in good hands. If you have any problems with my siblings, just call me."

"Will do," Gage said, even though he had no intentions of calling Stetson. He could handle the Kingmans for a couple weeks—even Adeline.

After Stetson left, Gage headed to the bunkhouse to take a shower. All the ranch hands had already left. Since they'd spent the night doing security for the wedding, Gage had given them the day off once their morning chores were done.

It was nice having the entire bunkhouse all to himself. He took his time in the shower, steaming some of the kinks in his back out that he'd gotten from sleeping on the scaffolding platform. Still, he preferred it to sleeping with a bunch of farting, snoring cowboys.

When he'd accepted the job of ranch manager, he'd asked Stetson if he could fix up the rundown house in the north pasture to live in.

But the house still needed a lot of work before it would be inhabitable. Gage had only had time to fix the roof before the trouble started on the ranch.

The hot water ran out, and Gage turned off the shower and dried off. He had plenty to keep him busy today and needed to get to it. But as soon as he stepped out of the bathroom, the door of the bunkhouse flew open and Adeline Kingman came marching in. She stopped short when she saw him. More than likely because he wasn't dressed in anything but his birthday suit.

Her gaze lowered, then quickly shot back up to his face. "Oh!" She whirled around, and he figured the assault on her tender sensibilities would have her scurrying right back out the door. But it appeared her panties were in too much of a bunch to leave. Although from the smooth fit of her tight jeans, he'd say she wasn't wearing panties. Or maybe a lacy pink thong that showed off her full, rounded cheeks.

Just like that, his cock started to rise.

It shocked the hell out of him. He was not attracted to Adeline Kingman—at least not after he'd met her. Thankfully, as soon as she spoke in her haughty voice, his body came to its senses. His semi-erection wilted like a deflated balloon.

"How dare you talk my brother into letting you run the ranch while he's gone?"

Gage pulled his gaze from her curvy butt. "I didn't have to do much talking. I just had to be the only logical choice."

Her shoulders visibly tightened, and he knew

she was pissed. He also knew that her voice wouldn't show it. It never showed any emotion. It was always cool and robotic. "Are you saying that you're a more logical choice than his own family?"

Since he hated talking to people's backs, he walked into the bathroom and grabbed a towel and wrapped it around his waist.

"You can turn around now. I'm decent."

She turned. Her gaze swept the length of his body and her cheeks flushed a bright red. He didn't care that he was embarrassing her. She wanted to walk into the bunkhouse uninvited, to hell with her. He crossed his arms over his bare chest.

"You were saying?"

She pulled her eyes back to his face and blinked. "I was saying that a man who has worked on a ranch for only a year is a ridiculous choice to take over while Stetson is away."

"I agree. But I haven't worked on a ranch for just a year, Miss Kingman. I've done ranch work all my life."

Her chin came up. "Where?"

"That's none of your business."

Her eyes shot daggers, but she kept her voice calm. "Wolfe, Buck, and Delaney have worked a ranch all their lives too. On a ranch I'm sure is much bigger than the ranch you grew up on."

It was bigger. But not by much. Still, he kept that information to himself. Just like he'd hidden the fact that he'd been a Marine.

"And what about you?" he asked. "I notice you

didn't include yourself in the list of siblings who work on the ranch."

"I've done ranch work, Mr. Reardon, if that's what you're asking."

"I find that hard to believe. Ranching is difficult to do from a tower room."

Adeline's blue eyes flared with anger. "How dare you judge me!"

"I'm not judging. I'm just making an observation. If you want to hide in your tower, that's totally up to you. But don't expect to promote confidence in your ability to run the ranch by playing Stetson's broken-hearted sister. Just like Wolfe should realize that getting tossed in jail doesn't make Stetson comfortable with leaving the ranch in his care. I think Stetson would love to be able to hand over some of the responsibility of running the ranch to y'all. He's just waiting for you to grow up enough so he can. From the looks of things, he's going to have a long wait."

Her eyes widened, and he figured he'd just royally pissed her off. Her mouth opened and then it closed. Then it opened again. But no words came out. Probably because all the words she wanted to say weren't fitting for a prim and proper princess to say.

"Go ahead," he taunted. "Call me every name in the book. I know you want to. I promise not to tell a soul that you aren't the sweet perfect woman everyone thinks you are."

She looked like she was about to explode, and he thought for sure he was going to hear at least a "Go to hell." Instead, she turned on a designer boot heel and stalked out the door.

Once she was gone, Gage couldn't contain his smile.

Putting Adeline Kingman in her place had been damn fun.

# Chapter Three

"REALLY, WOLFE? REALLY?" Adeline glanced over at her brother, who was sprawled out in the passenger seat of her Yukon, looking like a scruffy tomcat that prowled the streets at night. His long black hair was mussed, a layer of dark whiskers covered his jaw, his black t-shirt was ripped and wrinkled, and he had a shiner of a bruised eye.

"Really what? It's not like I haven't gotten tossed in jail before, Sis." Wolfe shot a glance over at her. "Although my siblings usually don't leave me there."

"I would've come sooner, but Stetson didn't tell me where you were until this morning. He thought a couple nights in jail would teach you a lesson."

Wolfe massaged his neck. "It taught me that the jail needs new mattresses and pillows. My neck is killing me."

She glared at him. "You deserve more than a few kinks in your neck. You deserve your butt kicked. You couldn't have waited until Stetson left for his honeymoon before acting a fool, Wolfe?

He almost canceled his trip because of you."

Wolfe stopped massaging his neck and looked over at her. "But he didn't, right?" He glanced at her hands on the steering wheel. "Hey, you got your cast off."

She flexed her wrist. Before bailing Wolfe out of jail, she'd gone to her doctor's appointment. He'd declared her wrist healed and removed her cast. After weeks of having the cast on, it felt strange to be without it.

"Yes, I got my cast off," she said. "And no, Stetson didn't cancel his trip. He and Lily left first thing this morning. But he wanted to cancel it. And if anyone deserves a vacation, it's Stetson. You know how hard he worked to keep the ranch going after Daddy passed away."

Wolfe snorted. "All hail Saint Stetson."

"Don't you dare take that tone, Wolfgang Kingman. Not when Stetson has the huge responsibility of keeping our family together. Do you think it was easy for a twenty-year-old college kid to take on the running of a huge ranch and the responsibility of four insolent teenagers?"

"You have never been insolent, Addie. You're as much of a saint as Stetson. It's the three younger Kingmans who got all the piss and vinegar."

Wolfe was wrong. Adeline wasn't a saint. On Judgment Day, she'd have a lot to atone for. No matter how many sins Wolfe had committed, they didn't come close to being responsible for a man's death. But rather than argue, she kept her mouth shut as her brother continued.

"I don't think having to put up with me, Buck,

and Delaney has been easy. And I appreciate all Stetson has done. But I'm not as saintly as you and Stet. Some of us are just selfish human beings who want to enjoy life before we end up in the grave. Which seems to happen to our family at a young age. If I'm going to die early, I want to live first."

Wolfe had a point. Longevity didn't run in their family. Most of their ancestors had died before they reached their mid-fifties. Their grandparents on their mother's side had died in a private plane crash at fifty-three and fifty-four. Grandma Kingman had died of breast cancer at forty-two. Grandpa "King" Kingman of a heart attack at fifty-one. Their mother had died in a car accident when she was only thirty-two. And their father of a heart attack—like his father—right after his forty-seventh birthday.

She glanced over at her brother. "Is that why you're always going hell bent for leather? You're worried about dying young?"

Wolfe touched the bruised skin beneath his eye and winced. "I'm not worried about it. I just think our family history should teach us a lesson about living life to its fullest. And that's what I intend to do. I won't work myself into an early grave like Stetson seems to want to." He grabbed the dashboard as Adeline took a curve. "Although I might be in that grave today if you don't slow the hell down."

Adeline let up on the accelerator. "But I thought you loved working the ranch."

"I do. But I enjoy other things too. Like women,

whiskey, and a good bar fight."

"Was a bar fight worth Stetson's trust?"

He stopped touching his eye and looked at her. "What do you mean?"

"After you called Stetson to bail you out, he decided you couldn't handle running the ranch while he's away. So he left Gage Reardon in charge." She expected the news to upset her brother the same way it had upset her. But she'd never been able to predict Wolfe's reactions.

He slumped back in the seat and sighed. "Thank God. I was not looking forward to two weeks of being the boss of a bunch of rowdy cowboys, doing boring paperwork, and having to deal with Buck and Delaney's constant bickering."

"So you don't care that Stetson gave the job to someone who isn't even a Kingman?"

Wolfe laughed. "You sound so snobby, Addie. Gage is a good guy and a damn good rancher. Why would you care if he's in charge of the ranch for a couple weeks?"

"Because he's an arrogant ass."

Wolfe stared at her with surprise. She wasn't prone to cussing. When she did, it got her siblings' attention. "Why do you think that? Did he say something rude to you, Addie? Do something inappropriate?"

She really wanted to tell Wolfe about Gage grabbing her in the garden and strutting around naked in front of her. Of course, the naked part hadn't been his fault. She was the one who had busted into the bunkhouse.

It had been a huge mistake. Now she couldn't

seem to get the image of Gage's naked body out of her head. Men used the term "built like a brick shithouse" for women. But Gage actually was built like a brick shithouse. His body was made of brick after brick of thick, sturdy muscle all mortared together with smooth, tanned skin.

"Addie?" Wolfe cut into her thoughts, and she realized she hadn't answered his question.

"No, he wasn't rude or inappropriate. He's just so full of himself. He thinks he's the better choice to run the ranch than Stetson's own family."

Wolfe relaxed back against the seat. "He's right." When she flashed an annoyed look at him, he laughed. "I get that you'd rather have someone from your family running things while Stetson is away. But Gage really is the better choice. Buck and Delaney are too immature. I'm too irresponsible. And you are . . ." He let the sentence drift off.

She stared at him. "I'm what?"

"Well, you're a little lost." He glanced over at her with sad eyes. "It's been over a year, Addie. Don't you think it's time to let Danny go and move on?"

He was right. She did need to let Danny go. But it was hard to do when she felt responsible for his death.

Wolfe glanced out the window. "Would you slow down? You're going to drive right past Nasty Jack's, and I need to get my truck. And pay Jasper for a few broken items." He flashed her a grin. "You wouldn't happen to have any money on you, would ya, sis?"

It turned out Wolfe had broken more than a few things during the bar fight. The bill Jasper handed her was for over six hundred dollars.

"Come on, Jasper," Wolfe said. "Couldn't you give me the family discount?"

Jasper Kingman was their second cousin. His grandfather was King's brother and the only person in Adeline's family who had lived past middle age. Uncle Jack was close to eighty and he was as mean and nasty as the name of his bar suggested. Adeline often wondered how Jasper could stand working for his grumpy grandfather.

"Don't just stand there yakking, Jasper!" Uncle Jack yelled from the corner table where he always sat. "This ain't no social hour. Get that bar polished up."

"Yes, sir." Jasper sent Wolfe and Adeline an eye roll before he went back to polishing the bar with a rag and beeswax. "Sorry. If it were up to me, I wouldn't charge you at all."

"We'll be happy to pay for any damages," Adeline said. "Wolfe wants to take responsibility for his actions." She shot a stern look at her brother. "And apologize."

Wolfe shrugged. "Sorry, Jasper."

"And to Uncle Jack," Adeline said.

Wolfe sighed before he turned and headed over to Uncle Jack's table. When he was gone, Adeline looked back at Jasper. "Can I bring you a check tomorrow? I don't have that much cash on me."

"Sure." He grinned. "If you can't trust family, who can you trust? It's not a big deal. It wouldn't be Saturday night if someone didn't get into a fight." He scooped more beeswax out of a can and rubbed it into the wood of the bar. "So did Lily and Stetson get off okay? I know Stetson hated to leave what with all that's been going on. Any luck finding out who messed with the brakes on his truck?"

"No. And Sheriff Dobbs has been absolutely no help. I'm surprised he even showed up here the other night to deal with the fight."

Jasper laughed and continued to polish the bar. "I guess Wolfe didn't give you the details of what happened. It was Sheriff Dobbs who Wolfe got in the fight with. Wolfe accused him of not doing his job and Deputy Tater jumped in to defend Dobbs and shoved Wolfe into a table. And we all know what happens when you get physical with the wolf man." He grinned. "He knocked Tater out cold with one punch."

Adeline shook her head. "Well, that explains why he landed in jail. He's lucky the sheriff and deputy didn't file charges."

"They aren't stupid enough to get on the bad side of the Kingmans."

Few people were willing to go up against the Kingmans' power and money. Sheriff Dobbs had gotten into office because Stetson hadn't cared one way or the other about who was sheriff as long as they didn't interfere with the Kingman Ranch. But after the way the sheriff had handled the accident that had almost killed Stetson and Adeline, Stetson was no longer indifferent toward Sheriff Dobbs. Come election time, Adeline didn't doubt for a second that Stetson would back whoever ran against Dobbs. And they'd win.

But in the meantime, Dobbs wasn't doing anything to stop whoever was out to get Adeline's family. Thankfully, Stetson had hired a private detective to help figure it out. According to Stetson, the detective had asked Jasper to put together a list of everyone he remembered being at the bar the night of Adeline and Stetson's accident. Suddenly, Adeline wanted to see that list.

"Did you ever get the list put together for the detective Stetson hired?" she asked.

Jasper stopped polishing the bar. "Yeah, but I don't know how complete it is. The bar was packed that night and it's hard to remember everyone who was here. I keep adding to it when I remember someone else."

"Do you think I could have a copy?"

"Sure. I'll be happy to make you one." Jasper left and returned only moments later with a copy of the list. It was long.

"Thanks, Jasper. I appreciate it." Adeline folded it and slipped it inside the pocket of her purse next to the bill for the damages. "And sorry about the fight."

"No problem, cuz." Jasper winked at her.

After Adeline and Wolfe left the bar, Wolfe checked under the hoods of both their vehicles to make sure no one had tampered with anything.

"Everything looks okay." He slammed the hood of her Yukon. "Still, you need to slow down—" He cut off when he glanced over her shoulder. "Shit. It's Kitty Carson. Let's get out of here before she—damn, too late."

Adeline turned to see Kitty's mail truck zip into the parking lot and come to a dust-spitting halt. Kitty hopped out with a big buck-toothed smile.

"Why, Wolfe Kingman, I thought you was in jail."

Wolfe pinned on the charming smile he always used with women. "Good mornin', Miss Kitty. My, my, aren't you lookin' like a ray of sunshine today." He held out his arms. "As you can see, you can't believe everything you hear."

Kitty placed a hand on her ample bosom. "Well, I'm glad to hear it. Just like I told Myra Evans, it would be a crying shame if one of the Kingmans turned out to be a bad seed." She shook her head. "Just a cryin' shame."

Wolfe leaned closer. "I am a bad seed, Miss Kitty. Just don't tell anyone."

Kitty swatted his arm. "You stop your teasin', Wolfe Kingman. You're not a bad seed. You're just sowin' a few wild oats." Her gaze moved over to Adeline, and her eyes welled with tears. "Adeline. How are you doin', hon? I swear my little ol' heart just aches for you every time I think of you waitin' for your hero to come home so you two high school sweethearts could live happily ever after." She sighed dramatically. "And then you got that call from his mama." Her voice cracked. "It's just a cryin' shame. Just a cryin' shame, I tell you."

Thankfully, before Kitty burst into tears—or Adeline did—Mystic Malone arrived. Mystic ran the hair salon in town, Cursed Cut and Curl, out of the basement of her grandmother's palm reading and fortunetelling business. Unlike her family, Mystic couldn't read the future in cards or palms. But she could tell what hairstyle would look best on you. And whether your hair needed highlights, a trim, or deep conditioning.

"Hey, Addie!" Mystic gave her a hug, then looked at Wolfe. "I heard you were causing some problems at Jack's on Saturday night."

Wolfe's eyes widened. "Me? Cause trouble?"

Mystic laughed. "Don't you play innocent with me, Wolfe Kingman. Buck has filled me in on all your wild escapades." Buck and Mystic had gone to school together since they were in kindergarten and were best friends.

"All exaggerations," Wolfe said. "I'm just a good ol' country boy trying to enjoy life."

Mystic rolled her eyes. "Sure you are." She looked at Kitty. "Hey, Miss Kitty. I hope I'm not interrupting anything, but I need to talk with Adeline about the Cursed Ladies' Auxiliary club's next charity fundraiser." Mystic was the president of the club. "You don't mind if I steal her away, do you? You're more than welcome to come along if you want to. I know my grandmother would love to see you."

That was an out-and-out lie. Everyone in town knew that Hester Malone and Kitty Carson did not get along. Hester thought Kitty was a gossip and Kitty thought Hester was a witch.

Kitty shook her head. "Thanks, hon, but I need to get back to delivering the mail." She glanced at Adeline. "But I'm glad you're going to be helping out with the fundraiser. It's about time you got back to life." She shook her head as she hopped into her truck. "A cryin' shame. Just a cryin' shame."

When she was gone, Adeline smiled at Mystic. "Thanks for saving me."

"No problem. I figured you didn't need to listen to Debbie Downer's dramatics. And I really did want to get your opinion on our next fundraiser. With the prom coming up, we thought we'd sell used prom dresses. We started asking for donations and I wanted you to take a look at the gowns and see if you think it will be worth the trouble."

Adeline didn't want to be pulled into the fundraiser, but she couldn't bring herself to say no. "Of course." She looked at Wolfe. "Do you want to come?"

"I'll just wait here."

Mystic laughed. "Scared Granny might read your palm and see wedding bells in your future?"

Wolfe shivered. "Hell yeah, I am."

"Chicken," Mystic called over her shoulder as she and Adeline headed down the street to the Malone house.

While most of the townsfolk's homes had suffered one calamity after another, the Malone's two-story farmhouse had never even had a gust of wind take off a shingle. It was the oldest house in Cursed and had survived Indian attacks, tornados, hail, freak blizzards, and even a Civil War skirmish. Some folks believed it had to do with the family's connection with the spiritual world and that unnamed forces protected it. But most people thought the clapboard structure had just been "built damn good" by Grandpappy Malone.

Before Mystic and Adeline could even get to the steps of the front porch, the screen door swung open and a woman with silver hair that fell in waves all the way down to her waist stepped out. Hester Malone was in her late sixties, but looked no more than fifty-five. Adeline had to wonder if there were metaphysical forces that protected her skin from the elements like it had protected the house.

"Adeline Kingman." Hester moved toward the steps. The long black flowing dress Hester wore made her appear to be floating on air as she moved to the edge of the porch. She held out a hand that was covered in rings like a queen greeting a visitor to her palace.

Adeline quickly climbed the steps and took her hand. "Hello, Ms. Hester. How are you?"

"I'm fine. But you're not." Hester spoke in an eerily soft voice. "Last night, I had a dream." She clutched the large purplish crystal that hung from a chain around her neck and closed her eyes. "I dreamt a dark cloud moved over Kingman Ranch, snuffing out all light."

This wasn't news. As much as Stetson tried to keep it a secret, most of the townsfolk knew about the trouble on the ranch. Still, Adeline didn't want to be rude by pointing that out.

"Thank you, Ms. Hester. I appreciate the warning."

The older woman held up her hand. "That's not all."

"Hessy, please," Mystic cut in. "If people want

their fortune told, they'll ask. Otherwise, you need to keep your gloom and doom to yourself."

Hester lifted an eyebrow at her granddaughter. "It's not gloom and doom. One day, you'll understand the burden of the gift the Malone women have been given."

Mystic rolled her eyes. "Believe me, I know all about carrying burdens, Hessy."

Ignoring her, Hester looked back at Adeline. "The black cloud came from the sooty breath of an evil dragon. A dragon disguised as a knight in shining armor. This villain waited until Stetson's back was turned before he struck with his razor sharp teeth."

Adeline's heart started to race. "Are you saying someone is going to kill Stetson?"

"My dreams only foreshadow the future. Stetson might not die, but his life is in danger. And what this man has planned will take Stetson completely by surprise. He's someone your brother trusts and views as a friend. Someone who has full access to everything Stetson cherishes." She paused. "Luckily, a hero arrived in my dream and revealed the dragon for who he is."

"Who?" Adeline asked. "Who is the hero?"

Hester smiled. "You, Adeline. You're the hero."

# Chapter Four

*A HERO?*

All the way back to the ranch, Adeline couldn't stop thinking about Hester's words. The woman had to be reading more into her dream than there was. Adeline was no hero. She could barely get through each day. Like Wolfe had pointed out, she was lost. Totally and completely lost. She was struggling to find her way out of the dark cloud that had consumed her. It wasn't just Danny's death. It was the role she'd played in it.

Hours before Danny had died, she'd broken up with him. He'd been upset. She'd heard it in his voice. No matter what the military had told his parents about Danny being killed by enemy fire, Adeline still felt responsible. If she had only waited until he'd gotten home to tell him she no longer wanted to marry him, maybe he would've been more alert and seen the danger.

No, she was no hero. Hester had misinterpreted the dream. Maybe the hero who came to Stetson's rescue had been Delaney. That seemed much more likely. Delaney could easily slay a dragon.

And yet, Mystic's grandmother had been adamant that it was Adeline who saved the day. Riding up on a white stallion, she had vanquished the dragon with her sword. The dream sounded more like an episode of *Game of Thrones* than a prediction of the future. If it had been anyone else but Hester who'd had the dream, Adeline would've dismissed it easily.

But Hester's predictions were rarely wrong. She'd predicted numerous tornados and ice storms long before the weathermen's reports, giving the townsfolk plenty of time to prepare. She'd predicted that Grady Clines would win a state senate seat when Grady had been a long shot. She'd predicted Milly Davis would marry Mac Jenkins, even when Milly and Mac had always fought like cats and dogs. And she'd predicted plenty of other things that had all come to pass.

But she'd also predicted plenty of things that hadn't come to pass, including the prediction she made Adeline's senior year of high school. Adeline and some of her friends had thought it would be fun to go to have their palms read to see what their futures would hold. Hester had given the other girls vague predictions about marriage and job opportunities. But when she'd looked at Adeline's palm, she'd grown intent.

"There is more sadness in your future, but your days of sadness will come to an end when you marry your soldier."

But Adeline hadn't married her soldier. If she had, Danny probably wouldn't be dead. If Hester had gotten that wrong, maybe she'd gotten the dream all wrong as well.

But what if she hadn't?

What if Adeline *was* the only person who could save Stetson and the ranch? If she stood by and did nothing and something happened to her brother, or any of her siblings, she would never forgive herself. She couldn't even forgive herself for Danny. She needed to do something. Maybe she should talk to the investigator Stetson had hired.

Unfortunately, she didn't know his name. She called Wolfe, but he didn't know it either. And neither did Buck and Delaney. Obviously, Stetson didn't trust them enough to relay the information. She couldn't blame him. Gage was right. The Kingman siblings had sat back and allowed their big brother to handle everything to do with the ranch, instead of stepping up and helping him.

Which was why she refused to call Stetson for the investigator's number. He deserved to have a vacation free from worrying about the ranch. She couldn't chance him cutting his honeymoon short and coming home. She could find the number. He probably had it written down somewhere in his office.

As soon as she got back to the ranch, she headed to Stetson's study to look. But when she reached the open doorway, she stopped short.

Gage sat behind her brother's desk.

"What are you doing here?" she asked.

Gage looked up from the laptop screen he'd been studying intently. "Where have you been, Miss Kingman?"

"That's none of your business. Now answer my

question. What are you doing here going through my brother's files?"

He leaned back in the chair, placed his hands behind his head and stretched, causing his biceps to flex. An image of him naked popped into her head. She quickly blinked it away as he spoke.

"If I'm going to run the ranch while your brother is gone, I need to access his files . . . with his full permission." He lowered his arms. "Now where were you? I thought Stetson made it clear that you weren't supposed to leave the ranch without Wolfe or Buck."

"I was with Wolfe."

"Not when you left the ranch. Buck said he saw you leave alone." When she saw Buck, she was going to give him hell. Gage easily read her anger. "Buck was worried," he said. "He doesn't want anything else happening to you. He realizes that next time, you might not just end up with a broken arm and a few bruises." He glanced at her wrist. "I see you got your cast off."

She moved into the room. "And I see you still don't get that just because Stetson put you in charge of the ranch, doesn't mean you're in charge of me."

He studied her for a long moment. "You're right. If you want to put yourself in danger, it's your business. But you need to realize that if something happens to you while Stetson's gone, it doesn't just affect you. It affects the trust Stetson has placed in your brothers . . . and in me. Now if you'll excuse me, I have work to do." He returned his attention to the laptop screen, completely dismissing her.

It galled her to no end that he was acting like she was intruding on him when this was her house. It also galled her that he was right. If something happened to her, Stetson would blame Buck and Wolfe. And they'd blame themselves.

But she wasn't going to leave until she got what she came for. And seeing her brother's laptop made her realize Stetson had probably been communicating with the investigator via email. All she had to do was check his email contacts.

She stepped closer to the desk. "I need to use Stetson's laptop. Just for a second."

"Why?" Gage continued to type.

The red mark on one of his fingers drew her attention. It was a bite mark. Her bite mark. The sight of it made her feel guilty and . . . suddenly extremely warm. The guilt she understood. She didn't like hurting anyone or anything. But the heat that consumed her at the sight of the bite mark made no sense. She could not be sexually attracted to such an annoying man. And yet, the tingly feeling that settled deep inside her was definitely sexual.

Which thoroughly annoyed her.

"I don't have to tell you why I want to use my brother's laptop," she snapped.

Gage sighed, clicked a few more keys, and then got up from the chair. "Fine." He waved a hand at the chair. "Help yourself." He propped a shoulder against the wall and crossed his arms.

"Aren't you going to leave?"

"Nope, I still have some paperwork to finish."

She glared at him, but didn't argue. It was a waste of time to argue with a Neanderthal. She came around the desk and took the chair, trying to ignore him. It was extremely difficult. Especially when the scent of horses, hay, and hardworking man enveloped her. She tried not to breathe through her nose as she looked at the screen of the laptop. He had closed the files and logged out. Which meant she would need to log back in.

"What's Stetson's password?" she asked as she poised her fingers over the keyboard.

"You don't know your own brother's password?" It was easy to read the smugness in his voice.

She gritted her teeth. "No. Now what is it?"

"I'm sorry, but if you don't know it, I can't give it to you."

She spun the chair around. "Just give me the password!"

A smirk spread over his face. "I'm afraid I can only do that with Stetson's permission."

Adeline didn't know exactly what happened. The control she'd been holding onto for months—or possibly years—snapped. One second, she was just sitting there, and the next second, she had jumped up and grabbed hold of Gage's t-shirt. "Give me the damn password, you arrogant asshole!"

She thought he would be shocked by her outburst. She certainly was. But he didn't act shocked. His smirk turned into a full-blown smile. "So the ice princess does have some fire."

Ice princess? Rage was too mild a word to describe the feeling that boiled over inside her.

"I'll show you fire, you cocky cowboy. Get out of my brother's office. Now!" She tightened her fist in the soft cotton of his shirt and tried to pull him toward the door, but it was like trying to move a redwood tree. He didn't budge an inch. As his smile got bigger and more annoying, she jerked harder and harder on his shirt, trying to move the unmovable ... until, with a loud rip, she ripped the t-shirt right off his body.

Thrown completely off balance, she went tumbling back. But before she could crash into the desk, Gage reached out and grabbed her.

Once again, she found herself pressed against him. But this time, he was half naked. She didn't know a man's skin could feel so hot. And yet, it didn't burn. She felt like she had just been submerged in a bathtub of warm water after a chilly walk in the cold autumn rain. Being surrounded by his heat didn't just warm her outside, it also caused a warm glow to build inside. It had been a long time since Adeline felt warm inside. Too long.

His hands tightened on her waist. "Adeline?"

It was the first time he'd ever used her first name. With his smooth east Texas accent, it didn't sound like her own. It sounded different. Special.

She tried to speak, but she couldn't. Not when feelings of desire were fluttering around inside her like a swarm of butterflies released from their cocoons. But it couldn't be desire. The last person she wanted to feel desire for was Gage Reardon.

It had to be something else. Disgust. Annoyance. Hate.

The sundress she wore was backless and Gage's hand rested on her bare skin, each calloused fingertip branding her like five red-hot coals. When they shifted in a soft caress, the feeling tumbling around in her belly intensified.

It was definitely desire.

Dammit.

She closed her eyes, trying to fight the overwhelming tide of emotions that seemed to be sucking her under. Right when she almost had her body under control, something happened to send her spiraling again.

Gage kissed her.

Where his body had warmed her, now his lips incinerated her. They lit her up like dry kindling and set her ablaze with need. A need she had never felt before. Never. At the moment, she would do anything to fill that need.

Anything.

Her arms went around his neck and she pulled him closer, taking over the kiss with a hungry swirl of her tongue. He moaned deep in his throat, the sound vibrating through her mouth like a mating call. She melted against him, wanting to be absorbed into his hot skin. But before she could get more of Gage, a surprised intake of breath cut through her sexual haze.

"Oh, beg pardon. I didn't realize this room was occupied."

Adeline drew back from the kiss and stared at Gage for one stunned second before she stepped out of his arms and turned to the housekeeper, who looked as embarrassed as Adeline felt. Gretchen Flaherty's round cheeks were as pink as the gingham print of her apron.

"I'm so sorry, Miss Kingman. I didn't mean to interrupt. I'll just let you get back to . . ." Gretchen waved her feather duster. "Whatever y'all were doin'."

Even though she was completely shaken by what had just happened, Adeline was somehow able to pull herself together and speak. "It's fine, Gretchen. Mr. Reardon and I were just . . . discussing ranch business."

Behind her, Gage snorted. But, thankfully, Gretchen ignored him.

"Of course." She placed a hand on the doorknob. "I'll just close this so no one else—"

"No!" Adeline yelled so loudly Gretchen jumped and dropped her feather duster. Adeline lowered her voice. "I mean there's no reason to close the door. Mr. Reardon and I are finished here." She moved around the desk on wobbly legs, hoping to escape before she was stuck with Gage. Alone. She should've known he wouldn't let her leave without being a jerk.

"Miss Kingman?"

She halted, but didn't turn around. "Yes?"

"Are you forgetting something?"

"I'll use Stetson's laptop later."

"I wasn't talking about the laptop. I was talking about my shirt."

Adeline glanced down at the ripped cotton she still clutched in her fist, and her cheeks flamed.

Not with embarrassment as much as anger. He could've let her leave without bringing up his shirt. He wanted to humiliate her in front of Gretchen. Well, she wasn't going to give him the satisfaction.

"Of course, Mr. Reardon." She wadded it up in a ball and threw it at him. It hit him square in his face. Unfortunately, it didn't wipe off the smug smile.

He caught the shirt before it hit the floor. "Thank you, Miss Kingman." He looked down at the tatters in his hand. "Although it looks like it belongs in the rag bag." He moved around the desk. "If you ladies will excuse me, I better go find myself another shirt."

Adeline glared at him as he passed, hoping to communicate just how much she loathed him. Either he couldn't read her message or he didn't care. The smile never left his face.

Once he was gone, Adeline couldn't keep her feelings in a second longer. "I despise that man. Totally and completely despise him." She turned from the doorway to see Gretchen staring at her in confusion. She understood why. She was feeling more than a little confused herself. Moving behind the desk, she flopped down in the chair and covered her face with her hands. "I don't know what happened. I don't know why I kissed a man I despise."

Gretchen spoke in her deep southern drawl. "As my mama always says, 'Love makes about as much sense as a dog climbing a tree.' Take my old boss and his wife for example. They never have a kind word to say about each other. But they have eight kids and would've had more if his wife hadn't had to get her female parts removed. So I figure they don't always hate each other. And maybe a little hate makes things a lot spicier."

Gage's kiss had been spicy. Adeline's lips still tingled. Maybe Gretchen was right. Maybe hate was as passionate an emotion as love. Or even more passionate.

She lowered her hands. "Still, I shouldn't have kissed Mr. Reardon."

"Why not?" Gretchen picked up her feather duster. "If I had the opportunity to kiss that hot cowboy, I'd sure take it."

Adeline laughed. When she'd first hired Gretchen as their housekeeper, she'd worried about her being so outspoken. But over the last few weeks, Adeline had discovered there was something about Gretchen's blunt honesty that was charming. Probably because Adeline was just the opposite and kept everything bottled up tight. She wished she was more like Gretchen and could say what she felt.

"Thank you for making me feel better," she said.

"Any time." Gretchen's expression grew serious. "And don't you worry about me tellin' a soul, Miss Kingman. What happens in this house stays in this house."

"Thank you. And like I've said before, please call me Adeline or Addie. You might work for me, but that doesn't mean we can't be friends."

A big smile spread over Gretchen's face. "I'd like

that . . . Addie. Now I better get back to work." She hesitated. "And if I was you, I'd chase Mr. Reardon down." She winked. "Before he finds a shirt." She fanned the feather duster in front of her face. "Lordy, that man has one fine body. And that sexy tattoo . . . ooh-wee."

Adeline remembered seeing the colorful ink on Gage's back as he walked from the room. But she'd been too angry to pay attention to what it was. Gretchen hadn't been as distracted.

"I've seen a lot of tattoos in my day," Gretchen continued. "But never one like that. It looked like it landed right on his back with its tail winding down his spine and those wings stretched across his shoulder blades. It was the most realistic fire-breathing dragon I've ever seen in my life."

## Chapter Five

"Now I've had about enough of your foolishness, Gage Liam Reardon. You need to get your butt home and you need to get your butt home now."

Gage sighed and rubbed his temples. This was a conversation he had with his grandmother on a regular basis. It was exasperating . . . and heartbreaking.

"It's been over a year," Nana continued. "I know what you went through had to be tough. I get that you aren't feeling quite yourself. But I don't get why you need to be away from your family in order to get better. Being surrounded by people who love you is what helps you get through your worst times."

That was the problem. His family thought they could help him, but they couldn't help him fight all the demons he'd collected while in Iraq. If he went home, he knew his Nana, his mother, two sisters, and aunts would be fretting over him like mother hens while his grandfather, father, brothers, and uncles would be buying him beers and urging him to talk about things. The week he'd spent at home after getting out of the military had been hell. Everyone stared at him with sympathetic eyes as if they were waiting for him to lose it. Which made him want to lose it. And he refused to take out his guilt and anger on his family. He'd planned to be gone from home for just a few months. Just until he'd met the girl who had broken Danny's heart and he'd confronted her with what she'd done. He'd wanted to look Adeline in the eyes and tell her about Danny's last hours on the face of the earth. He'd wanted her to know how devastated he'd been by her rejection. How heartbroken and gutted. He'd wanted her to feel heartbroken and gutted too.

But when he'd met the ice princess, he'd known that telling her about Danny's last hours wasn't going to make her feel anything. Adeline didn't seem to feel. When he found that out, he should've gone home. But it turned out to be much easier being a lone drifter than a mentally wounded war hero.

At the Kingman Ranch, he was just expected to do a good job. At home, he was the son, brother, grandson, and nephew his family wanted to be happy. The rest of his family had accepted that he needed time. Nana never would. She wanted her youngest grandchild home and couldn't understand why he wasn't. Gage had learned it was best not to make promises he couldn't keep.

"I'll be home soon, Nana."

"When?"

Maybe sooner than he wanted. For most of the day, Gage had been waiting for a call from Stetson firing his ass. Or for Wolfe and Buck to show up in the stables to kick his ass. But it was close to seven p.m., and he hadn't received a call or an ass kicking. Which meant that, once again, Adeline hadn't said anything to her brothers.

He wondered why. It was quite obvious that the kiss had ticked her off. At least, she'd been pissed afterwards. During the kiss, she'd seemed quite . . . enthusiastic. So enthusiastic that Gage had a hard time connecting the passionate woman he'd held in his arms to the cold, frozen princess. He now understood why Danny had fallen head over heels. There was fire beneath the ice.

Gage needed to stay away from that fire if he didn't want to get burned like Danny had.

"When, Gage?" Nana repeated her question. "I want an exact date so I can make plans."

Gage knew exactly what kind of plans his grandmother wanted to make. She had been trying to get him married for years. If it wasn't one of her friends' granddaughters, it was a "sweet little gal" she'd met at church. And Nana made no effort to hide her matchmaking plans.

"There's someone special I want you to meet," she said.

He sighed. "Like I told you before, Nana, I'm not ready to get into a relationship."

"Who said anything about a relationship? I want you happily married. And don't tell me you're not ready. You're almost thirty. You're practically middle aged. You remember that sweet little gal from church I was telling you about? Well, she up and fell in love with the preacher's son and they eloped last weekend. If you keep it up, all the good women in this town will be taken and you'll become a crotchety old bachelor like your great uncle Willy."

Gage couldn't help but grin. He loved his feisty grandma. "Uncle Willy might be crotchety, but he seems content enough with his life."

"Content? Who wants to be content? Just ask him about the gal he let get away because he was too selfish to grab love by the horns when he had the chance."

Why an image of Adeline popped into his head, Gage didn't know. Or maybe he did. He should've let the girl get away. But when his fingers had touched skin that wasn't cold to the touch, but soft and warm, he'd completely lost his head. He'd forgotten who she was and what she'd done. He'd forgotten she was Stetson's sister and his job was to watch out for her.

But he wouldn't forget again.

"There you are, Gage." Buck peeked over the stable door. "I've been looking all over for you."

Gage got up from the turned over feed bucket he'd been sitting on and spoke to his grandmother. "I have to go, Nana. I'll call you tomorrow."

"Don't you dare hang up on me, Gage Liam, until you give me a date."

"Soon. I promise." He ended the call and slipped his phone in his back pocket before opening the stall door. "What did you need, Buck?"

"Nana?" Buck grinned. "And here I thought you were hiding in an empty stall to talk to a girl."

"Last time I checked, my nana is a girl."

Buck laughed. "You know what I mean. Of course, I should've known better. You're all work and no play. And speaking of play, I need some in a bad way." His smile faded. "It's Delaney. She's driving me to drink, Gage." He took off his hat and slapped it against his leg. "I'm telling you, I can't take it anymore."

Unlike most twins, Buck and Delaney fought like cats and dogs. Gage wanted to believe that beneath all the arguing, the brother and sister truly loved each other. But, after listening to their squabbling for the last year, it was getting harder and harder to believe.

"What did she do now?" Gage moved from stall to stall, giving each thoroughbred horse a goodnight pat on the withers. He didn't know if the horses cared one way or the other about his nightly ritual, but he did. Horses soothed him like people never could. Which was one of the reasons he'd stayed so long at the Kingman Ranch. The other was that the Kingmans reminded him of his own family.

Buck followed close on his heels. "She brought one of her baby goats into the house and I found the kid in my closet chewing on my brand new ostrich boots."

Delaney loved animals more than anyone Gage had ever met. Since Gage had a soft spot for them too, he couldn't really blame her. "I'll talk with her."

"Talking won't do any good. I've talked until I'm blue in the face." Buck shook his head. "She's a spoiled brat who doesn't listen to anyone. She didn't even listen to Daddy. Of course, he never did get after her or Adeline. They were his little princesses who could do no wrong. I understand him thinking that about Addie. She's sweet as the day is long. But Del is no princess. She's the devil incarnate."

Delaney did do whatever she wanted without any thought to the consequences, but Gage knew Adeline wasn't as sweet as her family thought. She had pulled the wool over their eyes. But she didn't fool him. His body might've reacted to her soft skin and sweet curves, but his brain knew better.

"Just take over for a few hours, Gage," Buck broke into his thoughts. "I just need a few hours at Nasty Jack's or I'm going to go insane."

"After what happened with Wolfe, I don't think Nasty Jack's is a good idea." Gage scooped up some oats and offered them to Glory Boy. The thoroughbred foal would be leaving with his new owners soon and Gage would miss him. He'd been here for his birth and felt a special bond with the baby horse. Usually the foal ran right over when Gage leaned into his stall and offered him oats. Tonight, he seemed completely disinterested in the treat.

"That was just Wolfe's temper," Buck said. "I'm a lover, not a fighter."

Gage opened Glory Boy's stall and moved closer to the foal to check out his mouth and eyes. Both looked normal. Maybe Glory just wasn't in the snacking mood tonight. Still, Gage intended to keep an eye on him. The foal was worth a fortune and he didn't want anything to happen to him. He gave the oats to Glory's mother, Magnolia Breeze, before he moved out of the stall and continued his conversation with Buck.

"I'm not just worried about you getting into a bar fight. You know what happened to Stetson's truck at Nasty Jack's." It had been at the bar that Stetson's brakes were tampered with.

"That's because he didn't think to lock his truck so no one would have access to the engine without setting off the alarm. I'll make sure to lock mine."

Gage wished it were that simple. "I doubt that whoever tampered with Stetson's brakes will try the same thing again. He'll try something different. Something just as sneaky. And no one can defend themselves against a sneak attack." He could tell by Buck's stubborn face that he wasn't getting through to him so he tried a different angle. "And I don't know why you'd want to head to Nasty Jack's when there's a poker game tonight in the bunkhouse."

Buck frowned. "Because Delaney's playing poker Last time, she took everyone's money and then strutted around like the cock of the walk for the next few days." He shook his head. "It's not just cards she thinks she's the best at. She thinks she's better at everything. All of the guys are sick and tired of her competing with them. You should ban her from the bunkhouse and stables. I'm telling you, it would be the best thing for morale."

"You and the other cowboys are just upset because Delaney usually wins. You and I both know she's a damn good ranch hand. I figure she's earned the right to do a little bragging."

Buck sighed. "So I guess you're not going to give me a break from her."

Being in charge of the Kingmans for a couple weeks was becoming a much bigger pain in the ass than Gage had thought. "Fine. You head on over to the bunkhouse and I'll see if I can't talk Delaney into hanging out with me for a few hours."

It wasn't difficult to get Delaney to change her plans. All Gage had to do was call her and tell her about Glory Boy.

"I hate to take you away from the poker game, Del, but Glory Boy is acting a little strange. I wanted you to take a look and see if you thought I should call the vet."

"Of course! I'll be right there."

Since a few months earlier Lily had been attacked by a masked man in the garden, Gage didn't want Delaney walking to the stables by herself. He quickly headed to the house. Knowing how much Delaney hated to feel like she was being guarded, he waited for her behind the shrubs that lined the path leading to the back door. Only a few moments later, he heard the door open and Delaney stepped out.

Unfortunately, she wasn't alone.

Adeline stepped out with her. She'd changed from the sexy sundress she'd worn earlier to black yoga pants that hugged her long legs and curvy hips, and an oversized sweatshirt. She looked like she'd been getting ready for bed. Her face had a rosy just-scrubbed look, and her hair was piled up on top of her head in a messy bun. The white-gold waves caught the last rays of the setting sun and tempted a man to bury his nose in the soft nest to see if it smelled like sunshine. He shook the thought away as Adeline and Delaney's conversation reached him.

The two sisters rarely fought, but they seemed to be arguing now.

"I didn't think I had to worry about you being my babysitter too, Addie," Delaney said. "Believe me, I have plenty of those. I can't go anywhere without Buck or Wolfe following me."

"They should be with you now," Adeline said. "You shouldn't go to the stables alone."

"Like I told you, I won't be alone. Gage will be there."

"That's the problem. I don't want you anywhere near Gage."

"But you won't tell me why. Did Gage do something to you?"

Before Adeline could tell her sister about the kiss, Gage stepped out from behind the shrubs and took off his hat.

"Good evening, ladies."

"Hey, Gage," Delaney greeted him with a bright smile. Adeline, on the other hand, wasn't so happy to see him. Of course, she never was. But tonight she didn't give him her usual frosty look. Tonight, the look she gave him was more . . . terrified. Her eyes were wide and she had grabbed Delaney's arm in a death grip. "Oww, Addie." Delaney pulled free. "What's the matter with you?"

Gage wanted to know the same thing. Why was she looking at him like he was a villainous monster who was going to pounce on her at any second? Had the kiss in the study scared her? She certainly hadn't seemed scared. In fact, she'd shot daggers at him as he'd walked out of the room. Now, there were no daggers. Just unmitigated fear. It made him feel guilty as hell when he had nothing to feel guilty about. Yes, he had kissed her, but she'd fully participated.

Still, he couldn't ignore her fear.

"Why don't you stay with your sister, Del," he said. "It looks like she doesn't want you to leave tonight. I can handle calling the vet for Glory Boy if I need to. Where's Wolfe?"

"He's sleeping like the dead after his time in jail. And Buck is no doubt already losing all his money at the bunkhouse." Delaney looked at Adeline. "Is that why you're acting so weird, Addie? You're worried that no one will be around to protect you?" She patted Adeline's arm. "It's okay, sis. I'll hang with you tonight. I just need to check on Glory Boy real quick and then I'll be right back. I'm sure Gage will be happy to watch out for you while I'm gone."

"I don't think—" Before Gage could even finish the sentence, Delaney was striding down the path toward the stables. He planned to follow her, but first he needed to set things straight with Adeline. He turned to her and she backed up like he was going to attack her.

He held up his hands. "Look, if this is about what happened in the study earlier, you can relax. There won't be a repeat."

That didn't make the fear leave her eyes. She visibly swallowed. "Who are you?"

"Excuse me?"

"Where did you come from? Why did you choose this ranch to work at?"

So Adeline had figured out that he hadn't just happened upon the Kingman Ranch. Gage was surprised. He thought if anyone would find out about his deception it would've been Stetson. Certainly not his sister, who seemed more wrapped up in herself than anyone else. But she didn't have the details and he wondered what—or who—had tipped her off. Until he knew, he wasn't about to confess.

"I choose this ranch because you breed and train the best thoroughbred cutting and racing horses in the country. And I happen to like horses. As to where I come from, I've lived in a lot of places before I got here." It wasn't a lie. He had been stationed in a lot of places the eight years he'd served in the military.

"You said you've done ranch work for most of your life. Where? What ranches?"

She had him there. If he said the Sagebrush Ranch, she could easily Google his name and the ranch and find out who he was. And he wasn't quite ready to leave the Kingman Ranch.

"Why all the questions, Miss Kingman?" he asked.

"Because I want to know the type of man who's working for me."

"I don't work for you. I work for Stetson."

"And does he know who you are?"

"He knows me well enough to give me the job of taking care of his ranch while he's gone. Something he didn't even trust his own family to do."

The fear was gone now and anger flared in her eyes, turning them an even darker shade of blue. "Because you have him, and the rest of my family, completely fooled. But you don't have me fooled, Mr. Reardon. You were at Nasty Jack's the night Stetson and I were in the accident. And yet you never once mentioned it."

He stared at her as he realized what all her fear was about. "Wait a minute. You think I'm the one who has a vendetta against your family?"

"All the pieces fit. You were at Nasty Jack's the night Stetson's brakes were tampered with. You were right on Lily's heels when she ran to the house after getting attacked in the garden. You own a black hat and a red bandana. And you attacked me in the labyrinth the other night."

Gage was completed stunned by the accusation. Then he was pissed. Yes, he'd kept a few secrets, but he wasn't a cold-hearted criminal. "You're wrong, Adeline," he growled.

She pulled out her cellphone. "Then you won't mind if I call the sheriff and tell him my suspicions."

If it had been any other sheriff, Gage would've let her make the call. No sheriff in his right mind would arrest anyone on such circumstantial evidence. But Sheriff Dobbs was an idiot. The man might just side with Adeline and toss Gage in jail. While jail would be better than dealing with the crap Gage was having to deal with, he couldn't leave the ranch with no one in charge and the real criminal still on the loose.

He grabbed the phone out of Adeline's hands before she could finish dialing. "You're not calling the sheriff."

Her eyes widened, and she backed away. "I knew it. I knew you were the dragon."

The dragon? Before he could figure out what she was talking about, she turned and ran back to the house. He cussed and ran after her. He caught up with her in the kitchen as she was reaching for the phone. He grabbed her around the waist and lifted her off her feet.

"Stop this, Adeline. You're wrong."

"If I'm wrong, then why are you keeping me from calling the sheriff?" She elbowed him hard in the stomach and slipped out of his arms. He caught her by her sweatshirt and she turned and swung at him. "Let me go!"

"Not until you calm down."

"I'm sick of being calm!" She reached out and grabbed a pan that was hanging above the stove. Before he realized her intent, she hit him right upside the head.

He saw stars.

And then nothing but black.

## Chapter Six

"What's happening?" Gretchen came running into the kitchen in her chenille bathroom robe and fuzzy slippers. She came to an abrupt halt when she saw Gage sprawled out at Adeline's feet. "You killed Mr. Reardon."

Adeline was worried about the same thing. She hadn't intended to kill him. She'd just wanted to call the sheriff and protect her family. But now she was responsible for two mens' deaths. She dropped the pan and covered her mouth with her hand.

"What have I done?"

Gretchen hurried over and picked up the pan. "Let's not panic. My mama always says 'Nothin' good comes from panickin.' We'll figure something out." She chewed on her bottom lip. "Maybe we can bury the body before any—"

Wolfe slid to a stop in the doorway of the kitchen in his stocking feet and a pair of faded jeans. He looked down at Gage, then his eyes moved to Gretchen, who still held the frying pan. "What the hell did you do?" He turned to Adeline. "I told you she had a few screws loose and you should fire her."

Gretchen gasped. "You want me fired?" Before Wolfe could answer, she fled from the room.

Adeline would have gone after her if she hadn't been so worried she'd killed Gage. She dropped to her knees and felt for a pulse. The rhythmic throbbing in his neck had her sighing in relief.

"He's alive." She ran her fingers through Gage's thick hair and discovered a large lump on the side of his head. "Get me some ice, Wolfe."

While Wolfe did her bidding, Gage's eyes fluttered open. "What happened?"

Before she could answer, Wolfe came back with a plastic bag filled with ice. "Our loco housekeeper hit you with a frying pan."

"She didn't do it. I did." Adeline took the ice bag from Wolfe and shifted so Gage's head rested on her lap. She carefully pressed the ice bag to the bump, cradling his chin with her other hand. His scruff tickled her palm and made her breath hitch.

"You hit Gage with a frying pan?" Wolfe said. "Why would you do that?"

The confusion left Gage's eyes. They narrowed on Adeline. She shouldn't have knocked him out, but she wasn't wrong about him causing all the trouble on the ranch. Too many things pointed to his guilt. But if she really believed he was responsible, then why was she sitting there with his head on her lap as if he was an injured hero instead of a vanquished villain?

Before she could figure out her strange reactions to the man, he pushed her hands away and sat up. "Because your sister has been playing detective and believes I'm the one responsible for tampering with Stetson's brakes, attacking Lily, and every other bad thing that's happened on the ranch."

Wolfe laughed. "You're kidding, right?" When no one joined in with his laughter, his humor faded and he looked at Adeline. "Where would you get that crazy idea, Addie?"

"It's not crazy." She got up and tossed the bag of ice on the counter. "All the pieces fit. He owns a black hat and a red bandana. He was right there after Lily was attacked. And he was also at Nasty Jack's the night of the accident."

"Much earlier," Gage said. "I left long before Stetson showed up. And yes, I own a black hat and a red bandana, but so does every cowboy on this ranch—including Wolfe, Buck, and Stetson. I was close on Lily's heels that night because I was wide awake keeping an eye on the ranch and I heard her screaming."

All his excuses made sense. But a true criminal mastermind would have all his alibis ready. Adeline wasn't about to believe Gage so easily. "How do we know you left Nasty Jack's before Stetson got there? You could've hidden in the parking lot and waited for Stetson to go in before tampering with the brakes."

"I was here at the ranch when Stetson left for the bar. You can call and ask him. We talked before he left."

Since Gage being at Nasty Jack's was her main

piece of evidence against him, Adeline suddenly didn't have much to say.

"And there's another important piece missing from your case, Sherlock," Gage continued. "Motive. Why would I want revenge on a family I didn't even know until a year ago?" When she didn't have an answer, Gage snorted. "That's what I thought. If you're going to accuse someone of attempted murder, Miss Kingman, you need evidence. You can't make accusations because someone ticked you off." He picked up his hat from the floor. "Now if you'll excuse me, I've got work to do."

Once the door slammed behind him, Wolfe turned to her. "What are you doing, Addie? I get that you aren't happy about Gage being in charge. But accusing him of tampering with Stetson's brakes and attacking Lily is just crazy. Not to mention knocking him out with a frying pan. If he calls Stetson, you are going to be in deep shit."

Wolfe was right. Stetson would not be happy to hear about her actions. He might even cut his honeymoon short. All because Adeline had believed Hester's dream about a dragon. But it seemed like too much of a coincidence that Gage had a tattoo of a dragon on his back. And there were other things that didn't make sense.

"I wouldn't have hit him if he hadn't tried to stop me from calling the sheriff," she said. "That's suspicious. An innocent man would have nothing to hide from the law."

Wolfe snorted. "It's Sheriff Dobbs we're talking about. The man is an idiot. I wouldn't want you calling him either."

"But what do we know about Gage? I mean, he just showed up one day and Stetson hired him. A year later, he has full control of the ranch."

"He doesn't have full control, Addie. He has no control over the money or any major decisions. You know that. Basically, he's just doing what he's always done. Except now he has to deal with us. And that's not an easy job." He lifted his eyebrows. "Maybe you should give the guy a break." He yawned widely. "Now I'm going back to bed. If there's another crisis, call Buck or Delaney."

Adeline certainly wouldn't call Wolfe, that was for sure. He hadn't taken anything she'd said seriously. She couldn't really blame him. Her theory that Gage had caused all the trouble was pretty flimsy. She didn't have a motive or any real evidence. All she had was Hester's dream and a strong feeling that Gage wasn't telling the entire truth. Why was he so elusive about his past?

She heard a muffled sniff and turned to see Gretchen standing in the doorway. Her freckled face was all blotchy and her big brown eyes puffy. She held a stuffed tote bag in each hand.

"I just want to thank you for giving me a job, Addie. I enjoyed working here. I'm sorry I didn't work out."

Adeline hurried over and placed an arm around her shoulders. "You're doing a great job, Gretchen. You're the most enthusiastic, hardworking housekeeper we've ever had. There's no way I'm going to let you leave."

"But Mr. Kingman doesn't want me to stay."

"Wolfe says a lot of things he doesn't really mean. He was just surprised to see Gage sprawled out on the floor. That's all."

Gretchen sniffed. "Are you sure? Because he acts like he doesn't like me. I've tried extra hard to please him, but nothing I do seems to make him happy. He doesn't like me to bring him heated towels when he gets out of the shower. Or fluff up his pillows and fold down his sheets right before he goes to bed. Or slip up in the morning while he's sleeping to leave him his morning coffee."

Gretchen's determination to make Wolfe happy explained why he wanted her fired. He had been complaining for weeks about her showing up in his bedroom—and bathroom—unannounced.

"Wolfe is bit of a loner," Adeline said. "He doesn't like people making a fuss over him. The best thing to do is just ignore him and let him get his own coffee and towels."

Gretchen sniffed and wiped at her eyes. "So you really want me to stay?"

"Of course I do. Good housekeepers are hard to come by." Adeline took her suitcases away from her and set them down. "And so are good friends." She grinned. "Only a true friend would help you bury a body."

Gretchen glanced around. "I'm assuming Mr. Reardon is okay."

"Just extremely angry."

"Why did you knock him out with the frying pan?"

Adeline sat down on a barstool and sighed. "It's

a long story."

Gretchen took the barstool next to her. "I happen to like long stories."

Surprisingly, Adeline had no trouble confiding in Gretchen. She even told her about Hester's bizarre dream.

"Holy smokes!" Gretchen said. "That's why you looked so shocked when I described Mr. Reardon's tattoo. He's the dragon."

"That's what I thought, but I was just caught up in Hester's dream. There's no real evidence that points to Gage."

"But it can't be a coincidence he has a dragon tattoo and is extremely close to your brother. And the white princess certainly slayed the dragon. You knocked him out cold."

Adeline shook her head. "I almost threw up when I thought I'd killed him. I'm not a slayer."

"I think you're stronger than you think you are."

The vote of confidence made Adeline smile. "Thank you, but you're the only one who thinks I'm strong. Everyone, including my family, thinks I'm a fragile flower who needs to be protected."

"Probably because you act like a hothouse flower, hiding inside all the time." Gretchen placed a hand over her mouth. "Sorry, I shouldn't have said that. I have a problem where I talk before I think. I hope I didn't hurt your feelings."

Gretchen's words hurt, but only because they were true. "You're right. I have been acting like a hothouse flower and hiding away."

"That's okay. You just needed some time to get

over that beau of yours." Gretchen's eyes welled with tears. "I heard about him passing away. I guess you really loved him."

"Yes. I really loved him." *Just not enough. If she had loved him enough, she wouldn't have broken up him. Maybe he'd still be alive.*

Gretchen took her hand and squeezed it. "See. You are strong. If you conquered your grief over losing the love of your life, you can conquer a dragon."

"Gage might not be the dragon."

"But he could be. If he's not, then we need to figure out who is."

Adeline agreed. "Which is why I need to get ahold of the investigator my brother hired. He'll have a much better chance of getting information than I do." She nibbled on her thumbnail. "If I could only get into Stetson's laptop, I know I could find the investigator's name on one of his contact lists. But Gage is the only one with the password. He's not going to give it to me. Especially now."

Gretchen thought for a moment before her eyes lit up. "Maybe we could distract Gage while he's working and get him to leave the computer long enough so I could slip into the room and get it."

"I don't know, Gretchen. I hate to pull you into this. If Gage catches you, he could fire you. He is in charge."

"He won't catch me," Gretchen said. "I'm good at slipping in and out of rooms without people noticing."

Wolfe might not agree, but Adeline wasn't about to bring that up. "But how would I distract him? After I accused him and hit him over the head with a frying pan, he won't trust me."

Gretchen smiled slyly. "We don't need him to trust you. All we need is for him to want you. I think he already does."

"What do you mean?"

"I mean that men can't resist a beautiful woman. Even if they think it's a trap. Just look at Samson with Delilah. All you have to do is flirt with Mr. Reardon long enough for him to leave his computer so I can look at your brother's email contacts and get the investigator's name."

Adeline had never been one to use her female wiles to get what she wanted. And she didn't like women who did. But this was different. Her family was at stake. If Gage was a villain in hero's clothing, she needed to know so she could protect them.

Maybe the best way to slay a dragon was to seduce it.

# Chapter Seven

"How's Glory Boy this morning?" Delaney peeked over the stall door.

Gage continued to stroke the foal's back. "Not so good." Last night, he and Delaney had both thought Glory was feeling better. He'd nursed from his mother and started to perk up. This morning, he was back to not eating and acting lethargic. And Tab, the stable manager, said his feces were a little loose.

"We should probably call Doc," Delaney said.

"I already did. He's on a two-week vacation to see his grandkids in Alabama. The vet on call can't get out here until tomorrow or the next day. He thinks it's just something Glory Boy ate, and he'll be okay in a few days." He looked down at the foal lying on the bed of fresh straw Gage had just made for him. "Let's hope that's the case." He glanced behind her. "Where's Buck?" Gage didn't like Delaney wandering around the ranch alone.

"He's coming. I can't get rid of my lamebrain bodyguard for long. He's just talking with Wolfe about the excitement that took place last night." Her eyes twinkled with mischief. "Why didn't you tell me about what happened with Adeline? I thought you were acting all grumpy because I'd run off to the stables by myself. I didn't realize you were pissed off because my sister had cold-cocked you with a frying pan."

Gage was still pissed off. Not about being laid low with a frying pan, but about being accused of trying to harm the Kingman family when he'd been working his ass off trying to protect them.

Even a princess who didn't deserve to be protected.

"Your sister is loco," he grumbled.

Delaney's smile faded. "Hey, don't talk about my sister. I agree that she hasn't been herself since Danny passed away, but she's not crazy. She's just brokenhearted and depressed. She and Danny were childhood sweethearts and inseparable growing up. Everyone knew they were going to get married as soon as Danny left the military."

That had been the plan.

When Gage had first met Danny during Marine basic training in San Diego, he'd gotten to hear all about Danny's childhood sweetheart. Seven years later, when Gage and Danny were stationed together in Iraq, Gage had assumed Danny would already be married to his perfect woman. He hadn't been, but he was still madly in love with her. Hell, Danny's glowing descriptions of Adeline had Gage half in love with her. Those stories and the picture Danny kept pinned above his bunk.

In the photo, Adeline was dressed in a frilly prom gown with her hair cascading around her bare shoulders like a river of golden moonlight. Her deep twilight-blue eyes twinkled and her full lips were tipped up in a smile as if someone had just told her the funniest joke. She looked stunningly beautiful, but not in an untouchable way. She looked like a sweet girl next door. The kind who would welcome you home with open arms and loving kisses.

But Adeline didn't get a chance to welcome Danny home. A week before their platoon was scheduled to rotate out of Iraq, she had broken up with him over the phone. That night, he was killed during a routine night recon mission. Gage felt responsible. He should have told their commanding officer about Danny's state of mind after Adeline had broken up with him. He should have made sure Danny wasn't sent out with them that night. If Danny hadn't been so heartbroken and had been more alert, maybe he would be alive today.

"How's the old noggin, Gage?"

Gage snapped out of his thoughts to find Buck standing at the stall door with a smirk on his face.

"I guess my big sister is feistier than we all thought."

Gage wasn't amused. But the rest of the ranch seemed to be. Every cowboy he passed on the way to the house had a wiseass remark. When Gage stepped into the back door of the kitchen, Potts greeted him with the same smirk. Potts was the cook for the Kingmans. He was a crusty old cowboy who had no trouble speaking his mind.

"If you're gonna try kissing a gal, you might

want to make sure she's not holding a frying pan."

"I wasn't trying to kiss anyone." But he had kissed her. Even after she put a goose egg on the side of his head, he was having trouble forgetting that kiss. "I was trying to stop her from getting my ass tossed in jail because of some crazy theory."

Potts pulled a mug out of a cupboard. "Might not be so crazy."

"So you suspect me too?"

"I didn't say that." Potts picked up the coffeepot and filled the mug before handing it to Gage. "But I see why Adeline might. She doesn't know you like the rest of us do."

"Because she's spent the last year hiding away in her tower."

"With just cause."

Gage rolled his eyes as he sat down at the island. "Yes, I've heard all about poor broken-hearted Adeline who lost the love of her life." He took a sip of his coffee, then choked on it when Potts spoke.

"I don't think Danny was the love of her life."

After a long coughing fit, Gage cleared his throat and stared at Potts. "How do you know she didn't love him?"

Potts went back to scrubbing pans. "I didn't say she didn't love him. Addie loved Danny. They were two peas in a pod and the best of friends. I just don't think their friendship ever had the right passion to become anything else."

"Danny didn't believe that." Gage realized his mistake when Potts stopped scrubbing and turned to him. He tried to backpedal. "I mean from what I've heard. The entire town thought they were going to get married."

Potts went back to washing the dishes. "People only see what they want to see. Folks love the idea of childhood sweethearts tying the knot. I think the town's wishful thinking pushed Danny and Addie together more than any true feelings. The two of them probably would've figured that out if Danny had lived."

Gage wanted to argue the point. Not for Adeline, but for Danny. Danny had loved Adeline. He'd loved her with all his heart. There was no way he would've wanted to break things off with her. But he couldn't stand up for Danny without giving away their connection. So instead he let the subject drop and got to his feet.

"I better get to work. Thanks for the coffee, Potts."

On the way to Stetson's office, he ran into Wolfe. He waited for some smartass remark. Instead, Wolfe surprised him with an apology.

"Sorry about what happened, Gage. Adeline's not herself right now. And hanging around our crazy housekeeper hasn't helped. Anyway, I wanted you to know that I trust you and appreciate you taking over for Stetson. It's not easy running the ranch . . . or trying to keep an eye on the Kingmans."

That was an understatement. Gage couldn't wait until Stetson got back.

"Thank you, Wolfe." He started to leave, but Wolfe stopped him.

"There's not something going on between you and my sister, is there?"

Gage halted so suddenly he spilled coffee on his shirt. He turned to Wolfe. "Excuse me?"

"There seems to be a lot of tension between you and Addie. I just want to make sure it's not sexual."

Gage stared at him. "Sexual tension? Is that what you call getting hit over the head with a frying pan?"

Wolfe studied him for a long moment before he nodded. "Just making sure. Addie is a little vulnerable right now and I don't want her getting hurt again."

"I'm not going to hurt Adeline. In fact, I wouldn't need to be around her at all if you'd do your job of keeping an eye on her."

Wolfe nodded. "Will do."

But it turned out that Wolfe didn't get any better at his job. Only moments later, Gage was in the middle of reading an article about foal diseases when Adeline showed up . . . alone.

"Good morning," she said brightly—as if she hadn't tried to kill him the night before—and swept into the room without invitation.

Today, she wore a sundress like the one she'd worn the day they kissed. Except this one was more frontless than backless. The crisscross opening showed the swells of her breasts. His mouth suddenly went dry, and he took the last gulp of cold coffee before returning his attention to the article he was reading. Or trying to read. He couldn't concentrate when she moved closer and ran a finger with a pretty peach-colored nail along the top of the desk.

"What are you doing?"

He kept his eyes on the laptop screen, even though it had blurred out of focus. "Working."

She rested a hip on the edge of the desk. "So I guess you don't have time to help me."

He tried to ignore the leg swinging back and forth in his peripheral vision. "I have no desire to help a woman who tried to kill me."

The leg stopped swinging. She wore sandals with spiked heels that showed off her painted toes and the arch of her foot. "I wasn't trying to kill you. I only wanted you to let me go."

He lifted his gaze from her foot. "Because you think I'm a criminal who attacks women. And now you want my help? You really have lost it."

She jumped up from the desk. "I haven't lost it! Why do people keep saying that?"

"Because you keep acting like a nut. Start acting normal and maybe people will stop saying it."

"And exactly what is normal?"

"It's certainly not hiding out in a tower, sleeping on fountains, hitting people with frying pans, and accusing innocent people of heinous crimes."

Her eyes flared, and he thought she was going to attack him again. Instead, she took a deep breath and slowly released it. "You're right. I have been acting a little strange. And I probably should apologize. My siblings made me realize how bizarre my theory was. It's obvious that Stetson trusts you, and I trust my brother. So will you help me or not?"

"Help you with what?"

"There's a heavy box of old dresses at the top of my closet that I need to get down. I'm donating them to the Cursed Ladies' Auxiliary Club for their prom dress sale."

"And Wolfe won't help you?"

"He went out to the stables to check on Glory Boy." She hesitated. "How's the foal doing?"

"Why do you care? I haven't seen you in the stables once since I've been here."

She pressed her lips together. Lips he remembered kissing all too well. "Never mind. If it means I have to put up with your insults, I'd rather you didn't help me. I'll just ask Gretchen."

Asking the housekeeper to help with a heavy box had disaster written all over it. Gretchen was known for being more than a little clumsy. Even though Gage had sworn to keep his distance from Adeline for the rest of Stetson's vacation, he'd also sworn to protect her.

He stood and grumbled. "I'll get the box."

Adeline batted her eyelashes and spoke in sugary voice filled with sarcasm. "I'll be forever in your debt."

He followed her out of the office and up the long staircase. The dress was as backless as it was frontless, and he had trouble keeping his gaze off the soft skin it revealed. A strawberry-shaped birthmark sat right below her left shoulder blade. His stomach tightened with the sudden urge to lick it to see if it tasted like plump, juicy fruit. He pushed the thought away.

"My room is this way." She directed him down

the hallway. He'd never been upstairs before. It was as opulent as the downstairs with its marble floors, high ceilings, and rich paneling. He expected Adeline's room to be the same. A room fit for a princess with chandeliers, expensive knickknacks, and satin throw pillows. He knew she had a big four-poster bed with a canopy, but he hadn't been able to see the small details through his binoculars. So he was surprised to find the complete opposite of a princess's room.

The grandest piece of furniture was the bed, but there wasn't one satin pillow on it. Just an old fashioned quilt like the kind his Aunt Lucy and Aunt Gertrude made. The rest of the furniture looked like something you'd find in your grandmother's attic. There was a needlepoint rocker and a scarred chest of drawers. There were mismatched bookcases stuffed with all kinds of books.

Across from the bed was an antique dresser with a huge mirror that covered most the wall. Tucked into the frame were at least two dozen pictures. As Adeline led Gage farther into the room, he couldn't help stopping to look at the photos. Some were recent pictures of her and her siblings. Some were older pictures of them with their parents and grandparents. Adeline's mother had looked just like her. A stunningly beautiful woman with long hair the color of moonlight.

But the photos that grabbed Gage's attention the most were the pictures of Adeline and Danny. There were pictures of them as kids cuddling kittens on a pile of hay in a stall. Sitting on horses outside the stables showing off toothless grins. Holding up ribbons next to a cow. Standing on the railing of the paddock fence. And in front of a high school with their arms draped over each other's shoulders.

It was obvious they were close. But was Potts right? Had it been more of the friendship kind of love? At least on Adeline's side? If so, why had she continued to lead Danny on?

"The box is in here."

Adeline's voice pulled Gage's attention from the photos and he turned to see her disappear into a closet. When he followed her, he thought he'd find the walk-in closet filled with clothes, shoes, and purses. Instead, most of the shelves held books. Textbooks. He tipped his head to read a few of the titles and was surprised to discover they all had to do with veterinary medicine.

"Where did you get these?" he asked.

She glanced back at him, and her cheeks reddened. "I bought them."

"Why?"

She hesitated for a moment before she answered. "Because, at one time, I was interested in becoming a veterinarian."

A vet? He hadn't even thought Adeline liked animals. But the pictures he'd just seen told a different story. At one time, Adeline had loved being in the stables. What had changed?

"It's up there." She pointed to a large plastic container on the very top shelf of the closet. "Let me just get you the stepladder." She pushed back some clothes. "Shoot. The ladder's not here.

I guess you'll have to get one from the shed." She looked back at him and smiled. "If you don't mind."

"I do mind. I don't have all day to help you, Miss Kingman." He walked back out into the bedroom and grabbed the desk chair.

"I don't think that's a good idea," Adeline said when he walked into the closet with the chair. "That chair isn't very stable. I wouldn't want you to—"

Before she could finish, Gage had taken the box off the shelf and set it on the floor. "There you go." He started to exit the closet, but Adeline jumped in front of him.

"You can't leave."

"Why not?"

"Because . . . I need you to carry the box to my bed."

He blew out an exasperated breath before he picked up the box, which wasn't even that heavy, carried it out of the closet and plopped it on the bed. This time he didn't say a word as he headed for the door. Before he reached it, Adeline stopped him once again.

"Wait!"

Now completely fed up with catering to a spoiled princess, he whirled around and snapped. "What?"

She hesitated for only a second before she threw her arms around his neck and kissed him.

## Chapter Eight

ADELINE HAD NOT planned on kissing Gage. The plan had been to use a little flirting to get him to come up to her bedroom to help her get the box down while Gretchen got the information about the investigator from Stetson's laptop. And sending Gage to get a stepladder would've given Gretchen all the time she needed. But Adeline should've known Gage was too resourceful to fall for their plan. Since she didn't want Gretchen caught and possibly fired, she'd had to take drastic measures.

Like kissing a dragon.

For a second, she'd thought even that wouldn't work. His body tensed and his hands closed around her waist as if he was going to shove her away. But when his fingers brushed the bare skin of her back, instead of shoving her away, he tugged her closer and consumed her with the fiery, wet heat of his mouth.

He tasted of rich coffee and her reaction to his kiss was like a jolt of strong caffeine. Her body suddenly became fully awake, every nerve and cell aware of Gage like they had never been aware of another man. The hot slide of his lips. The rough brush of his tongue. The soft caress of his callused fingertips as they brushed over her naked back.

Beneath her hands resting on his neck, she could feel the strong throb of his pulse against her palms. The spot between her legs seemed to echo that pulse, sending shockwaves of need through her body. When Gage slid his hand in the front opening of her dress and encased her breast, that need swelled to overflowing.

She felt liquid. Like everything inside her had melted and she was being absorbed through Gage's mouth and fingers. She wanted him to absorb her completely. She didn't care if he was a dragon. All she cared about was the way he made her feel.

Alive.

Not dead.

She would have gladly let him consume her. But without warning, he suddenly released her and stepped away. He stared at her for a long second, his eyes confused and his breathing harsh, before he turned and walked out of the room.

She should've followed him to intervene in case he caught Gretchen. But her legs refused to cooperate, and she slipped down on her bed. A few minutes later, Gretchen appeared in the doorway. Adeline must've looked as dazed as she felt because Gretchen was immediately concerned.

"What happened?" Hurrying in, she sat down on the bed and took Adeline's hand. "Are you okay?"

Adeline nodded. "I just had to go to greater lengths than I thought to get Gage to stay here."

Gretchen's eyes bugged out. "Sex?"

"No! I just kissed him." Although if Gage hadn't stopped, she probably would've ended up having sex with him. She didn't understand how a man who possibly wanted revenge against her family could make her feel so alive. It made no sense. Danny had done a lot more than just kiss her, and she had never felt anything close to what she felt with Gage.

As if reading her thoughts, Gretchen smiled. "Well, the dragon must know how to kiss because you look like you've been thoroughly singed."

"It was worth it to make sure he didn't catch you."

"Oh, he caught me. He walked right in while I was still sitting at your brother's desk."

Adeline cringed. "Oh, no. Did he fire you?"

Gretchen shook her head. "He just said to tell you that you needed to work on your seduction skills."

Flopping back on the bed, Adeline stared up at the ceiling and groaned. "So the kiss was all for nothing."

"I wouldn't say that." Gretchen reached into her apron pocket and showed Adeline a business card.

Adeline sat up and took it. "It's the investigator's card. How did you get it?"

"I found it in the top drawer of your brother's desk."

"You mean all I had to do was look in Stetson's desk?"

Gretchen giggled. "But that wouldn't have been nearly as exciting. And you can't deny it's been an excitin' day. You have a sparkle in your eyes and a flush to your cheeks that wasn't there when I first came to this ranch. And I don't think it's all to do with Gage's kiss. I think you've found a purpose—protectin' your family from the dragon. Whether the dragon is Mr. Reardon or someone else, you can't stop until you figure out who he is. Like that fortuneteller said, you're the hero, Addie."

She hesitated for just a second before she picked up her cellphone from the nightstand and dialed the number on the card. Unfortunately, the investigator wasn't very helpful.

"I'm sorry, Miss Kingman. Your brother hired me and I can't talk to you about the case. That's confidential information."

"You don't need to tell me anything," Adeline said. "I just want you to investigate one of our employees. If you find anything suspicious, I want you to let my brother know immediately. I know you're probably already investigating everyone who works on the ranch, but I just want to make sure you thoroughly investigate Gage Reardon."

"Any reason?"

Since she wasn't about to tell him about Hester's dream, she hedged. "He just seems to always be around when things happen."

"I'll take care of it, Miss Kingman. Don't worry. I've got this covered."

After hanging up the phone, Adeline should've felt relieved about handing off the job of investigating Gage to a professional. But the investigator's condescending tone made her wonder if he would take the phone call seriously or if he just thought she was an overreacting woman.

"What are you thinking?" Gretchen asked. "I can practically see your brain ticking."

"I'm thinking we can't just leave Gage to the investigator."

Gretchen leaned in and spoke in an excited hushed voice. "So what's our next move? Should we ambush him, tie him up, and interrogate him?"

"Umm . . . I think that's a little extreme. But I do think we need to keep a close eye on him."

"But how do we do that when he spends most of his time at the stables?"

It was a good question. Since her siblings thought Gage could do no wrong, she couldn't ask them to help. And Gretchen had more than her fair share of work to do at the house. Even if she didn't, Gage would be suspicious if the housekeeper suddenly started hanging out at the stables.

That left one person for the job.

"I guess I need to get out my riding boots."

It wasn't like Adeline hadn't left the house in the last few months. She'd spent plenty of time in the garden. What she hadn't done was venture anywhere near the stables. And with good reason. The stables held all the memories of Danny. It was where they first met and where they'd spent the majority of their time.

Danny's father had been the ranch manager before Gage. Once Danny passed away, his father had quit—no doubt because the memories of his son had hurt him as much as they hurt Adeline.

The stables had been their own personal playground. As soon as the stables came in sight, all those memories came tumbling back in a huge tidal wave of sadness that threatened to pull Adeline under. Her heart started pounding in her ears and she struggled to draw a deep breath. She couldn't stay there. Not even to protect her family. But when she turned to head back to the house, she ran into a solid wall of muscle.

"So the princess does come out of her tower."

She kept her head lowered so Gage wouldn't read her panic and tried to step around him.

But of course the annoying man blocked her way.

"You want to tell me what you and your accomplice were looking for on Stetson's laptop? It must be something important if you were willing to kiss me to get it."

She wanted to say it was none of his business, but she didn't seem to have enough air in her lungs to speak. All that came out was a wheezy squeak.

Gage immediately lifted her chin and studied her face. "What's wrong? Are you having trouble breathing?"

"I-I-I'm fine."

"You're not fine." He pressed his fingers to the pulse on her neck. "You're heart is racing." Without waiting for a reply, he swept her up in his arms and carried her into the last place she wanted to be.

The stables.

Once inside, her panic grew. She fought to get out of Gage's arms.

"L-L-Let me g-g-go."

He set her down on a bench inside the door and crouched in front of her. "I want you to close your eyes and tell me three things you smell."

"W-W-What?" she panted.

"Close your eyes and tell me three things you smell." She started to argue, but he took her arms and squeezed. "Just do it, Addie."

She closed her eyes and tried to take a deep breath. It took a couple tries to get enough air in to actually smell. "I smell horse manure. And hay. And something fresh and clean like soap." Gage's soap. She had smelled it earlier when she'd kissed him. The memory of the kiss had heat infusing her face. She opened her eyes to find him looking at her lips.

He lifted his gaze. "Good. Now tell me three things you see."

The only thing in her line of vision was Gage. "You have a bigger splash of gold in your right eye than in your left."

"What else?"

Her gaze lower to his nose. "A bump on the bridge of your nose with a tiny scar."

"I got hit with a swing as a kid and had to have five stitches. Two months later, I did it again." He chuckled. "I've always been a slow learner." He encircled her wrist and lifted her hand. "Wiggle your fingers."

She complied.

"Wiggle your toes."

She tried, but it wasn't easy in her snug riding boots.

"Lift your shoulders."

When she finished lifting them, he pressed his fingers to her wrist for a long moment before he released her. "So you want to tell me what caused your panic attack?" Before she could come up with some excuse for her panic, he figured it out on his own. "The stables remind you of Danny. That's why you never come out here."

She stood. "Very good, Mr. Reardon. Now if you'll excuse me." But before she could escape, he got to his feet and took her hand, pulling her toward the stalls. "What are you doing? I don't want to stay here."

"I know what you don't want, Adeline. I also know what you need. Something that your siblings seem to ignore." He opened a stall door and pulled her inside before closing it behind them. She started to tell him to get the hell out of her way when a soft snort had her turning to the chestnut thoroughbred mare.

"Magnolia Breeze?"

The horse came over to greet her with a huffy breath and wet nose nuzzle. Adeline laughed and placed her arms around Magnolia's neck. "Well, hello, my gorgeous lady. Did you miss me? I missed you too. I heard you gave Majestic Glory a run for his money. Of course, you must've finally given in because I heard about your fine-looking son."

The horse drew back and bounced her head up and down as if in agreement. Adeline laughed and patted her neck. She glanced over to see Gage watching her.

"What?" she said. "Surprised that animals like me?"

"Actually, yes."

She rolled her eyes and returned her attention to Magnolia. She didn't notice the foal until he stuck his head out from beneath his mama's belly. "Well, there you are, Glory Boy." Adeline knelt down and waited for the baby horse to approach her. "My, you are a beauty. You look just like your daddy." The foal studied her with big brown eyes for a moment before he slowly came forward on long, spindly legs and allowed her to stroke his soft velvety forehead.

"Aww, sweet one. I don't know why Stetson agreed to sell you."

"I don't either," Gage patted the baby horse's withers. "He's going to be a champion cutting horse. Aren't you, boy?" It was easy to see that Glory Boy and Gage had a close connection by the way the foal allowed Gage to check his mouth and tongue.

"He looks like he's doing much better," she said.

"He seems to be. And I don't understand it. Yesterday, he was lethargic and wouldn't eat, but got better in the afternoon. Then this morning he wouldn't get up or nurse, but seems okay now."

"Maybe it's something he's eating?"

"That's what the vet thinks. But we've kept him on a strict diet and he hasn't been out to pasture. When we let him in the paddock to exercise, someone is always watching him."

"That is strange. Has he had all his vaccines?"

"Not yet. He was scheduled to get them this week. That's what has me worried."

It was something to worry about. There were all kinds of equine diseases that could kill a young unvaccinated foal. "You probably shouldn't give them to him until you figure out what's wrong."

"I agree." He stopped examining the colt and looked at her. "What stopped you from becoming a vet?"

She was surprised by the question. Not only because it came out of nowhere, but also because it wasn't something people had ever asked her. Not even her family. She understood. Stetson had been too busy with the ranch. And her siblings had been too busy being teenagers to be interested in their sister's career aspirations. But Gage seemed interested. His gaze was intent as he waited for her answer.

She cleared her throat. "My father passed away and Stetson had the huge responsibility of running a ranching business when he wasn't even out of college. He needed help. So I decided to quit school so I could help him with the house and keeping an eye on Wolfe, Buck, and Delaney."

"Not an easy task."

She smiled as Glory Boy came back over for attention. "It wasn't so bad. They aren't perfect, but they're my family."

"A family you gave up your dream for."

"Stetson did it. Why should I be different?"

Gage sat back in the corner and rested his arms on his knees. In his faded t-shirt and jeans, scuffed boots, and well-worn straw cowboy hat, he looked like all the other cowboys on the ranch.

Except all the other cowboys had never made her feel like she'd been plugged into an electrical socket. Gage emitted some kind of live current that Adeline couldn't ignore. It was there even now when he pulled out a piece of fresh hay from the feeder and stuck it in his mouth. A mouth she had kissed only hours before.

"From what I've heard, Stetson didn't give up his dream," he said. "He told me he always planned to take over the ranch. He just had to do it a little earlier than he expected. You completely gave up yours. Why?"

She looked away from the sexy cowboy image he presented and focused on petting Glory Boy. "Dreams change."

"Did yours?"

She couldn't answer the question. Mostly because she didn't know what she wanted anymore. At one time, she'd been so sure. She wanted to marry Danny and become a veterinarian and build a little house on the section of the ranch that her father had left her. Danny had always wanted to serve in the military. They melded their dreams together, deciding that Danny would become a Marine while she got her degree in veterinary medicine. Then they'd both come back to the Kingman Ranch and get married and have kids.

But then her father had died and she'd spent the next five years struggling with Stetson to keep the ranch going and the family together while Danny fulfilled his dream of serving his country. They talked and texted and saw each other when they could. But during those times when they weren't together, Adeline had started to notice other cowboys around the ranch. Which had made her question her feelings for Danny. When he'd called her one night from Iraq and told her he wasn't reenlisting and was coming home to marry her, she'd hesitated too long.

Why had she hesitated so long? Why couldn't she have just acted excited, then waited until he was safely home to tell him about her doubts? Instead, she'd been truthful and told him that she thought they should see other people before they made the decision to marry. Then fate had taken the decision out of her hands.

"Adeline?"

She looked at Gage and realized he was waiting for an answer. "Yes," she said. "My dreams changed."

Even if she hadn't wanted them to.

# Chapter Nine

IT HAD BEEN a huge mistake to get Adeline over her fear of the stables. At the time, he'd thought he was doing a good deed. Now, he knew exactly how Delaney felt when she complained about Buck following her. For the last few days, every time he turned around, he stumbled into Adeline. And not just in the stables. But also in the barn. At the paddock. Even when he saddled a horse and headed for the open range.

Stetson had told him that Adeline could ride, but Gage hadn't believed it until he saw it with his own two eyes. Not only could she ride as well as some of their best cowboys, she could rope, cut cattle from a herd, and jump a damn three-foot fence without losing her seat. And she did it all in jeans so tight they looked like denim paint.

He knew exactly what she was up to. She still didn't trust him. She was convinced he had it out for the Kingmans and was going to make sure he didn't do anything to her family on her watch.

And her watch was constant.

He glanced at his rearview mirror and shook his head when he saw Adeline's blue Yukon hugging the bumper of his pickup. Gage had thought coming into town to buy new socks and underwear would give him a break from her. Obviously, he'd been wrong.

Pressing down on the accelerator, he tried to lose her. But the woman drove like a maniac. On the last curve into town, she came so close to his bumper he thought she was going to drive right up into the bed of his truck.

It was the final straw.

He took the first street off the main highway, stopping right in front of the Malones' house. Sure enough, Adeline followed. When she pulled around him and parked in the driveway, he got out of his truck and stomped over to her Yukon.

"Stop following me."

She gave him an innocent look as she got out, one she'd been giving him a lot lately. "Following you? I am not following you."

"Then explain what you've been doing for the last few days."

She hesitated for a second, like she had her answer all ready. "I've decided to take a more active role in the running of the ranch. You're right. Hiding away in my tower hasn't instilled a lot of confidence in Stetson as to my ability to run the family business. So I'm changing that."

He lifted an eyebrow. "By becoming my shadow?"

"According to Stetson and all my siblings, you are the best."

"And following me into town is going to make you a better rancher?"

"I wasn't following you into town. At least, not on purpose."

He crossed his arms over his chest. "Uh-huh. Tell that to some other fool—"

Before he could finish, Mystic Malone came out of the front door of the house and waved. "Hey, Addie! Glad you could make it. You need help with anything?"

Adeline sent him a smug look as she called back to Mystic. "No. I can handle it."

Damn. He should probably apologize. Instead, he kept his mouth shut and watched as she walked around to the back of the Yukon and lifted the hatch. She really needed to get some looser jeans. When she reached in to grab a plastic container—the same container Gage had taken down from the shelf in the closet—Gage couldn't keep his eyes off the sweet curves of her ass.

She pulled container out and set it on the ground, then grabbed the other one and set it on top. She seemed to have no problem lifting both. After playing the weak damsel in distress, he should've let her. But his mama and Nana had done too good of a job of teaching him manners. Although he wasn't very gentlemanly about it.

"I'll get them." He snatched them out of her hands.

"My, but you are in a foul mood today." She slammed the hatch. "How's Glory Boy this morning?"

"Not eating again. And the vet had an emergency and won't be here until tomorrow. He's still not concerned." He paused. "I am."

"Me too," Adeline said. "I did a little research and maybe we should try deworming him. I'm assuming Doc did it at one to two months."

"He did. He planned on doing it again when he gets back from his vacation. But you're right. Maybe we should have the vet on call do it tomorrow."

"I can do it." He stopped and turned to her in surprise, and she laughed. "Yes, this princess knows how to deworm a horse."

"Well, come on, you two," Mystic yelled. "I'm not going to hold this door all day. What are you doing here, Gage? You lookin' to buy a prom dress?"

Mystic Malone was a big tease. Everyone in town knew it. Usually, Gage teased her right back, but today his mind was too preoccupied with Adeline wanting to deworm Glory Boy. She had surprised him a lot lately, and it left him feeling a little out of sorts.

"I'm just helping Miss Kingman," he said.

Mystic winked at Adeline. "Ooh, Miss Kingman, is it?"

Gage started to set the containers on the porch, but Mystic stopped him. "Don't you dare think you can run off without saying hi to the rest of the Cursed Ladies' Auxiliary Club, Gage Reardon. They'd never forgive me if I let a hot cowboy get away."

Once inside, Gage followed the two women through the house to a big screened back porch. Racks had been set up along the screens and in the center of the room and a gaggle of women were opening boxes of gowns and handing them to other women to hang. They all stopped when Gage entered.

"Sweet Lord!" Kitty Carson pressed a plastic hanger to her large breasts and gave him a bucktoothed smile. "If I'd known hot cowboys were invited, I would've changed out of my sweat shirt and yoga pants."

"I'd have changed out of my granny panties," Mildred Pike, who worked at the grocery store, said as she fanned her face with her hand. Mildred had the longest, scariest nails Gage had ever seen. They were always painted bright colors and decorated with little decals. Gage didn't know how she struck the keys of Cursed Market's old cash register, but somehow she managed.

Thelma Davenport was a large woman with a white streak running down the center of her short black hair. Thelma ran the only restaurant in town, Good Eats, with her husband. Otis was a big ol' boy who had been a linebacker for the New Orleans Saints before he'd gotten injured and moved to Cursed. He and Thelma had five grown kids and a bunch of grandkids. Thelma was always showing Gage pictures of those grandkids, but today she didn't seem to be in grandma mode.

She winked at him. "And if I'd known a cute cowboy was coming, I wouldn't have worn panties."

Her comment had all the ladies laughing. With three older sisters, Gage had been the brunt of female jokes all his life. He knew how to take it in stride. He placed the stacked containers on one of the tables and took off his cowboy hat.

"Good mornin', ladies. I'm sorry to disappoint, but I can't stay. Although I'd be happy to make a donation to the cause." He pulled out his wallet and took out all the cash he had on him and handed it to Mystic.

"Thank you, sir." She handed the money off to Kitty, who put it in a metal cash box on the table. "But we can't let you leave without a dress." She unsnapped the lid of the container he'd just brought in. She searched through the pile of dresses and pulled out one. "This one is perfect for you." She shook out the dress. "Don't you ladies think this pretty yellow one will go perfectly with Gage's blond hair and hazel eyes?"

Gage was caught speechless. This was the same dress that Adeline had worn in the picture Danny had pinned above his bunk. Gage didn't know if it was his emotional attachment to Danny that had him feeling gut shot. Or his emotional attachment to the damned photo. All he knew was the dress shouldn't be in a giveaway box. It shouldn't go to someone who didn't know what it had meant to a Marine.

To two Marines.

"You sold me." He went to take the dress, but his hand had just closed around the smooth satin when Adeline tried to pull it from his hand.

"I'm sorry, but I didn't realize this dress was in the box. I'm not giving it away."

Gage held tight. "But I just paid good money for it, Miss Kingman."

Adeline's eyes flashed with anger. "But you said

it was a donation, Mr. Reardon."

"That was before I saw the dress."

"This one's not for sale."

"And yet, I paid for it."

She gritted her teeth. "I'll give you your money back."

"I don't want it back. I want the dress."

They stood there glaring at each other until Mystic laughed.

"Now come on, you two, let's not come to blows over an old prom dress. If the dress is special to Adeline, you need to let her have it, Gage. I'm sure we can find you another dress that goes well with your eyes."

It didn't go well with his eyes. It went well with the angry eyes staring back at him. The combination of Adeline's blue eyes and the yellow gown had always made Gage think of a twilight sky hanging over the shimmering moonlit pond on his parents' ranch. Maybe that's why he felt so attached to the picture. It had reminded him of home when he'd desperately needed the comfort.

But he wasn't in Iraq now. He didn't need a picture or a gown. He needed to realize that and move on.

He let go of the dress. "Then of course, Miss Kingman should have it." With a tip of his hat, he headed for the front door. As he stepped out onto the porch, he thought he'd escaped all the women.

He was wrong.

"I'd be running for my life too."

He turned to see Hester Malone sitting in a

high-backed rocker on the front porch. He'd never met the town fortuneteller, but he'd heard stories about her and had seen her around town a time or two. She was a tall, willowy, silver-haired woman who dressed in black tops and matching flowing skirts. He'd never been close enough to see her eyes. They were the same violet-blue color as her granddaughter's. But whereas Mystic's twinkled with humor, Hester's were more solemn. And intense.

"It looks like you survived your foray into the chicken coop," she said. "They've been known to peck a rooster until there's nothing left but feathers."

Gage smiled at the metaphor. "I got out before they could do much damage."

"Smart man." She stopped rocking. "And a courageous one."

"The ladies weren't that hard on me. They were just having fun."

"I wasn't talking about your bravery facing the women of this town. I'm talking about your bravery serving our country." She stroked the large amethyst crystal that hung around her neck. "I saw you, you know. You were in a dream. Or I guess I should say two dreams. You're the warrior."

A tingle crept up his spine. It looked like Hester did know things other people didn't. Still, he tried to deny it. "No, ma'am. I'm just a cowboy."

She tipped her head and arched a jet-black brow that contrasted starkly with her silver hair. "What makes you think that cowboys can't be warriors?"

He shrugged. "I guess they can. But I'm just a cowboy. A cowboy who needs to get back to the ranch."

She got up from her rocker. Gage didn't know why he took a step back. Maybe he was a little freaked out by this woman.

"You're right," she said in a low, husky voice. "You do need to get back to the ranch. The dragon will strike again. In order to help defeat him, you must continue to be strong and vigilant. Your biggest battle is to come. You'll have to choose between loyalty . . . and love."

## Chapter Ten

"WELL, THAT WAS fun," Mystic said as soon as Gage left. "We should always invite a handsome cowboy to our meetings." She winked at Adeline. "Since most of the hot cowboys live on Kingman Ranch that will be your responsibility, Addie. Clothes are optional."

All the women laughed. Everyone but Adeline. She was still a little shaken by the dress. She hadn't remembered it was in the container. When Mystic had pulled it out, memories of prom night had flooded back.

She had been so happy then. Just a carefree teenager with no responsibilities or pressure. She and Danny had danced and drank the sloe gin Danny had snuck in his tuxedo pocket. After the dance was over, they'd driven to Prairie Pond and parked. Danny had slipped the dress off her and touched her in places no boy had ever touched her before. She'd waited for all the fireworks her friends had told her about to happen. But there had been no fireworks. Not even a wayward spark. And when Danny had attempted to have intercourse, she'd stopped him, using the excuse that she thought they should wait until they were married.

She stared down at the dress in hands. How foolish she'd been. How young, naïve, and foolish.

"Isn't that right, Addie?"

She blinked back her tears and looked at Kitty. "I'm sorry. What?"

"I said I'd take that hot cowboy any day. Even if he does have a fetish for women's clothing. Did you see the way he looked at that dress? 'Course, that probably explains why he doesn't have a girlfriend. Katy Hanks broke it off with Dave Melbourne when she caught him wearing her panties and bra. And poor Dave never did find himself another woman." She shook her head. "A cryin' shame, I tell you. A cryin' shame."

"I'm sure Gage didn't think he'd fit into that little dress," Mildred said. "I'm sure he wanted it for his girlfriend. A man who looks like that probably has plenty of ladies chasing after him. He's just smart enough not to date anyone in this gossipy town."

"Or maybe he and his gal are just good at keeping secrets," Thelma said.

"I doubt there's anyone that good." Mystic took the dress from Adeline and handed it to Kitty. "Hide this away so no one mistakenly sells it. Come on, Addie, you can help me get some refreshments."

Once they were in the kitchen, Mystic pulled a box of wine from the refrigerator and started filling the glasses that sat on the counter. "I'm sorry."

"For what?"

Mystic handed her a glass of wine. "For being such a smartass and pulling that dress out. I'm guessing it was one you wore with Danny."

Adeline nodded. "Senior prom. And you don't need to apologize. I should be getting over Danny."

Mystic turned and filled another glass. "You're here. I'd say that's progress. I still tear up every time I see a cat toy and Magic was just a cat. A darn cute cat, but just a cat. It has to be far worse to lose the love of your life. And you can't rush grief. But eventually, everyone needs to move on." She turned and leaned back against the counter, taking a sip of wine. "Now, tell me what's going on between you and Gage Reardon."

Adeline blinked at the quick subject change. "There's nothing going on between us. The man is just annoyed with me and decided to be a jerk about the dress."

"Annoyed about what?"

She hesitated before she told the truth. "I think Gage might be the dragon in your grandmother's dream."

Mystic choked on the sip of wine she'd just taken. When she recovered, she stared at Adeline. "You took Hessy's dream seriously?"

"Of course I did. Your grandmother has predicted a lot of things that have come true."

"She's also predicted a lot of things that haven't. That's why she doesn't have any friends in this town. And why I ignore dreams and any premonitions and keep my mouth shut."

"You have dreams and premonitions? But I

thought you didn't have your grandmother's gift."

"I don't. I don't have that gift and I don't want that gift." Mystic drained her glass. "The sight causes nothing but trouble." She pointed the empty glass at Adeline. "This is a perfect example. My grandmother has convinced you that someone close to your family is responsible for the crimes and now you think it's Gage."

"It makes sense. Only someone who has complete access to the ranch could've done all these things without being caught."

Mystic shook her head. "It's not Gage. He's angry at you for something, but I didn't get hate—I mean I don't feel like he hates you. And I don't feel like you hate him either, Addie. The sparks you two set off when you were fighting over the dress were purely sexual."

"Sexual?" Adeline shook her head. "I do not have sexual thoughts about Gage."

It was a lie. The more time she spent with him, the more she had sexual thoughts about him. No matter what Gage was doing—training cutting horses in the paddock, roping steers in the pasture, spreading straw in the stalls—Adeline couldn't keep her gaze from wandering over his hard body and wondering what it would be like to have it naked and stretched out on top of her. When they had been arguing over the dress today she couldn't help wondering what his lips would taste like if she leaned over and kissed him. The coffee and cinnamon roll Potts had given him that morning before he headed for Stetson's office? Or the mint gum he occasionally chewed?

Or the sweet hay he often plucked from a bale and stuck in his mouth?

Mystic's laugh pulled Adeline out of her thoughts. "Liar, liar pants on fire."

Before Adeline could wonder how Mystic had read her thoughts so easily, Kitty came into the kitchen. "Where are those refreshments? The girls are getting thirsty."

The prom dress sale was a huge success. They made enough to fund the charity Thanksgiving baskets with money to spare for the volunteer firemen's Christmas toy drive. Not only did the Cursed high school girls come to shop, but so did high school girls from all over the county. What they didn't sell that day, Mystic took pictures of and placed on Facebook Marketplace. She'd already had a dozen inquiries by the time everything was packed up and the patio furniture moved back to the screened in porch.

The weather had changed from a sunny morning to a dark, cloudy evening. Fat raindrops had started to fall as the ladies left the Malone house. Adeline hesitated on the porch, preparing for her race to the car, when Hester Malone came out.

"A bad storm's brewing."

Adeline smiled at the woman. "We can always use a good rain."

Hester's shook her head. "I wasn't talking about the rain. This will let up in a few hours. I'm talking about the trouble on your ranch."

After talking to Mystic, Adeline was having second thoughts about believing in Hester's predictions. But someone was out to get the

Kingmans. That wasn't a prediction. It was a fact. And until they were caught, it was hard to ignore Hester.

"Did you have another dream?" Adeline asked.

Hester rubbed the crystal. "This is more a dark feeling than a dream. It first came on me this morning when I saw Gage. He was the one I saw in my dream."

Adeline didn't know why she felt so stunned. She had thought Gage was the dragon and now her suspicions had been confirmed. Except, over the course of the last few days, her suspicions about Gage being the one responsible for everything that had been happening on the ranch had dwindled. In fact, they'd been almost completely snuffed out.

"Are you sure Gage is the—"

Before she could finish, Mystic came out the screen door. "Stop it, Hessy. I mean it. I've worked hard to keep friends in this town and I won't have you turning them to enemies with your foolishness."

"It's not foolishness. If Adeline is to prevail, she must be ready." Hester's eyes narrowed on her. "And be strong enough to confront the dragon."

"She's not going to confront any dragon. Now let her get home before the worst of this storm hits." Mystic hugged Adeline. "Drive safe, Addie. I'll call you later."

Adeline was a little too distracted by Hester having named Gage as the dragon to pay much attention to her drive home. Especially when she looked in her rearview mirror and saw Gage's truck following her. When she took the turnoff to the ranch, he drove even closer. Was this it? Was this when Gage revealed his true character and ran her off the road? He had the perfect alibi. Her brothers had always questioned her driving skills and the highway was slick like it had been the night Stetson's brakes had been tampered with. Had Gage done something to her brakes while she was busy selling prom dresses and was just following her to make sure, this time, he accomplished his goal?

She pushed the brakes and was relieved when the SUV slowed. Once she knew the brakes worked, she wasted no time getting back to the ranch. She pulled into the garage and closed the door, then hurried into the house, thankful to find Wolfe, Delaney, and Buck eating dinner around the kitchen table.

"Are you okay, Addie?" Buck asked when he saw her. "Your face is as pale as a baby's butt."

Delaney punched Buck on the arm. "Don't compare Addie's face to an ass, you ass." She studied Adeline. "But he's right. You do look a little peaked, Addie."

Wolfe got up from the table. "Did something happen?"

"No. Nothing happened." Nothing besides Hester's confirmation that Gage was the one she'd seen in her dream. And that wasn't real evidence of anything. Even Hester's own granddaughter didn't take the dream seriously.

So why did Adeline? Maybe because she liked the role she played in Hester's dream. Instead of a sad, depressed woman who spent all her time in her tower room, she was a hero. And she wasn't quite ready to let that role go.

When she got to her room, she sat down at her desk with her laptop. She hadn't found anything on Gage when she'd Googled him earlier, but maybe she needed to widen her search. Instead of searching Gage Reardon, she searched Reardon.

Unfortunately, there were a lot of Reardons in the United States. She added Texas and it slimmed down, but there were still an overwhelming number. Rather than look through every post, she switched the search results to images. It was much faster to scroll through pictures. Still, it was almost eleven o'clock before she found a photograph of Gage.

He looked much younger and much happier. A smile lit his face and his eyes twinkled beneath the brim of his cowboy hat. He had his arm slung around a pretty cowgirl. There were other smiling cowboys and cowgirls in the picture as well. They all stood beneath a ranch entrance sign.

Sagebrush Ranch.

The name sounded familiar. She clicked over to the website and quickly read the bio. Sagebrush was a huge cattle ranch. Adeline remembered Stetson mentioning it. Obviously, Gage hadn't been lying when he'd said he'd worked big ranches.

Adeline continued to scroll the bio and ran across a photo of the owners. Tate and Sally Reardon. Adeline studied the picture of the attractive older couple. Tate had Gage's features. Sally had

Gage's hazel eyes and blond hair.

If they weren't Gage's parents, they were certainly related to him.

Adeline was more confused than ever. Why would Gage come here to work when his family owned a ranch just as big? And why would he keep that information a secret and act like a cowboy drifter?

So much for Gage being a perfect saint. While she hadn't found any evidence that he was behind the crimes against the Kingmans, she now had evidence that he was a liar. There had to be a reason for his lies.

She hated to interrupt Stetson's honeymoon with bad news, but he needed to know what she'd discovered. But when she looked up the time in England, it was still too early in the morning to call. She would have to wait a few hours. She got ready for bed, but she couldn't sleep. Finally, she gave up and headed out to the balcony.

Hester had been right. The storm had moved on and the sky was completely clear. A fingernail sliver of moon hung amid the twinkling stars. She rested her arms on the railing and was about to wish on the brightest star that they would catch the person responsible for all the trouble on the ranch when she stopped herself.

No wishes. Wishes were for fools.

A moving light caught her attention. Not in the sky but close to the ground. She straightened and watched it move from the vicinity of the bunkhouse toward the barn. The same barn that someone had tried to burn to the ground.

She turned and headed back inside to get Wolfe and Buck, but then halted in her tracks.

If it was Gage, he would just say he was keeping an eye on things. If she wanted to prove he was guilty, she'd have to catch him in whatever nefarious act he was up to this late at night. And get it on video.

She hurried into her closet and tugged on a pair of cowboy boots, then pulled a black hoodie over her nightshirt. She grabbed the pepper spray out of her purse and slipped it and her cell phone in the front pocket of the hoodie before heading out the door.

It *was* dark outside. As she cut through the trees separating the barn from the house, she tripped and fell on all fours. She got up and brushed the mud from her hands and knees before she moved to the edge of the trees and looked at the barn. The light had disappeared. Had whoever it was gone into the barn?

She moved closer. After the barn had almost burned down, Stetson had locking steel doors with a security code installed. The doors were locked, the security pad blinking red. If he wasn't in the barn, where was he?

As silently as possible, she walked around the side of the barn and bumped into something. When she reached out and felt the cold steel, she realized she'd walked into the scaffolding that had been used to rebuild the roof. From the top of it, she'd be able to see most of the ranch.

Halfway up the scaffolding, she glanced down and wondered if this was the best of ideas. But she kept going. She couldn't help feeling a sense of accomplishment when she pulled herself to the top platform.

Her pride turned to fear when a deep voice spoke behind her.

"Doing a little sleepwalking, princess?"

## Chapter Eleven

GAGE WAS HAVING a bad day. He'd borne the brunt of the Cursed Ladies' Auxiliary Club, been warned by a fortuneteller of dark times to come, and got stuck in town babysitting Adeline. When he finally made it back to the ranch, he'd had to break up a fistfight in the bunkhouse and clean out Glory Boy and Magnolia's stall after the colt had diarrhea.

Once he'd showered, he'd climbed the scaffolding to make sure all was well on the ranch before he planned to get some shuteye. But obviously, his day from hell wasn't over yet. A disheveled princess was kneeling in front of him ... looking sexy as hell. Good thing he was too tired to feel even a tingle of sexual awareness.

Okay, so maybe there was a tingle. But nothing he couldn't ignore.

He crossed his arms over his bare chest and stared down at her. "Well? Do you want to explain what you're doing?"

She reached into the pocket of her black hoodie. For what, he wasn't sure. But whatever it was, she wasn't happy when she couldn't find it. She patted the pocket and then peeked over the edge of the platform before she looked back at him and audibly swallowed. "I was on the balcony and saw a light moving by the barn."

"And you thought it was a good idea to check it out yourself instead of asking Wolfe or Buck to do it?"

"Wolfe and Buck are right behind me."

He cocked an eyebrow. "Really? Buck!" he yelled. "Wolfe!" The only answer was the hoot of a night owl. He shook his head and sighed. "Go back to your tower, princess, where you belong. I'm too tired to deal with you tonight."

She stood. She should've looked ridiculous in the hoodie, short nightshirt, and boots. She didn't. Of course, Adeline could wear a gunnysack and look stunningly beautiful. With fire flashing in her eyes, she was even more so.

"Don't call me that! I'm not a princess. And I'm not leaving until you tell me what you're doing up here."

"My job. Which is keeping an eye on the ranch."

She lifted her chin. "Keeping an eye on the ranch? Or spying on the ranch?"

"I believe spying is your forte. That's what you've been doing that last few days, isn't it? Spying on the villain you think is out to get your family? And yet you don't have a shred of evident to support that theory."

She hiked her chin and sent him a smug look. "I do now. I know you're a liar, Gage Reardon of Sagebrush Ranch."

He wasn't surprised. With the way she'd been

following him around, he figured it was only a matter of time before she started doing some online research. He wondered how much she'd learned. Did she know he'd been a Marine? Or just that his parents owned the Sagebrush Ranch?

He held out his hands. "I guess you found me out. Now what? Are you going to have the sheriff arrest me for having a bigger bank account than you thought I had?"

"No. I'm going to call my brother and have him fire you for being dishonest. Once you're gone, I think the trouble on the ranch will end."

"There's still the problem of motive."

"That I haven't figured out, but it won't matter when you're gone."

"And you think if I wanted justice from the Kingmans that I'd let it go so easily? If you do, you don't know the first thing about revenge, sweetheart. Revenge for an injustice eats at a man's gut. Nothing will appease it but making the one responsible suffer."

Adeline's eyes widened. "Just what kind of justice do you want?"

It was on the tip of his tongue to tell her that he wanted her to feel some kind of remorse for breaking a good man's heart. But before he could, a loud crack rent the air. Growing up on a ranch, he was familiar with the sound of a bullwhip. He and his brothers used to have bullwhip contests to see who could crack theirs the loudest. But his father never let them use the whips around the animals. And whips on the Kingman Ranch were forbidden. So what was a cowboy doing cracking one in the middle of the night?

The answer to that question came in the sound of running hooves. Hooves that sounded like they were heading straight for the scaffolding.

"Shit!" He scooped a startled Adeline into his arms and made the leap to the barn roof. His bare feet slipped on the roof shingles and he fell on top of her. She screamed and pummeled his shoulders until the loud crash of falling scaffolding caused her to still.

She blinked at him. "What happened?"

"I would say that stampeding cattle just knocked down the scaffolding."

Her eyes widened. He knew how she felt. He was feeling a little stunned himself. He rolled off her and scooted to the edge of the steep roof. The scaffolding was nothing but a pile of metal and boards. There was no sign of the cattle. Or the person who had caused them to stampede.

Adeline joined him. Fearing she'd go tumbling off, he placed an arm around her waist as she peeked over the edge. "But I don't understand? I mean I get how they could've gotten out of the pasture. The ground is wet and muddy and they could've easily knocked down a fencepost. But why were they running?" She glanced up at the clear sky. "There's no lightning or thunder? What were they running from?"

"I wouldn't say what as much as who. The same person who was cracking the bullwhip."

Adeline drew back and looked at him. "I heard that crack. You're right. It did sound like a bullwhip. But why—" She cut off, and her eyes once again widened. "Someone was trying to get the cattle to stampede." She swallowed hard. "They were trying to kill me like they tried the night of the accident. And if you were on the scaffolding, that means . . ." She stared at him. "You're not the dragon."

"The dragon?" It wasn't the first time he'd heard the word that day. Suddenly, Adeline's suspicions of him started to make sense. "You went to the town fortuneteller to find out who was causing the problems on the ranch, didn't you?"

Her cheeks flushed a bright pink, and she looked away. It was all the answer he needed.

The mix of exhaustion, the brush with death, and the sheer absurdity of her thinking he was a dragon tickled his funny bone. He laughed so hard that he slipped a little closer to the edge.

"Be careful!" Adeline grabbed the belt loop of his jeans as if she could keep him from falling. "Stop laughing. It's not funny. All the pieces fit. Hester said the dragon was like a brother to Stetson. Stetson loves you like a brother and you happen to have a tattoo of a dragon on your back. It made sense."

"Believing a fortuneteller's dream makes sense?" He laughed even harder.

She released his belt loop. "Go ahead and fall, you fool."

He stopped laughing and squinted at her. "Who's the fool?"

She clenched her fists. For a second, he thought she might just shove him off the roof. But then she relaxed and sighed. "I guess I am. I shouldn't have accused a man of crimes just because of Hester's dream. But you are close to Stetson and you do have full access to the ranch and could've easily—"

All humor fled as he finished the sentence for her. "Attacked Lily and tried to kill you and Stetson? Thanks for thinking so highly of me."

"It's not like you think highly of me. You don't like me. You haven't liked me since you showed up at the ranch."

He couldn't very well argue. "I didn't accuse you of crimes." No, he'd just blamed her for his friend's death. Which he realized was just as undeserved. Adeline hadn't been the Iraqi who pulled the trigger. Deep down he had always known that. But he'd needed someone to take his anger out on. And maybe Adeline had needed that too. It would be a strange coincidence if they'd both used each other to get rid of the pain they felt after Danny's death.

For a moment, he thought about telling her that he'd served with Danny. But that hidden piece of his history probably would get him fired from the ranch. After what just happened, Adeline and her family needed protection more than ever.

"Come on," he said. "Let's get back from the edge before we end up in that tangled mess. Don't try to stand up. Especially in those slick-soled boots." He stayed behind her as she carefully crawled back up the roof. The nightshirt she wore barely cover her butt and every time she moved, he got a glimpse of panties riding high on her butt cheeks. Even after his brush with death, his dick proved it was still alive and well. It was a struggle to redirect his focus.

"Head up to the cupola. We can straddle the roof and rest against it until morning."

She stopped and glanced over her shoulder. "Until morning? We aren't staying up here the rest of the night."

"We don't have much choice. Unless you have a cellphone with you."

"I did, but it must've fallen out of my pocket when I tripped on my way to the barn. Don't you have one?"

"It's at the bottom of that rubble."

"Then we'll yell until someone hears us."

"Like they heard you screaming and the cattle knocking over the scaffolding? We're too far away from the house and bunkhouse for anyone to hear us yelling, Adeline. We have no choice but to stay up here until morning when Del or one of the ranch hands comes to feed the barn animals."

She didn't look happy about their situation. With a hard-on that could pound nails, he wasn't real happy about it either. But after only a second's hesitation, she continued to crawl up the roof. When they reached the peak, she straddled it. Her shirt hiked all the way up to the top of her thighs. Her legs in the cowboy boots looked a mile long. Trying to put as much distance between them as possible, he quickly moved to the other side of the cupola. But once he was leaning back against it, a thought struck him.

"You can't go to sleep, Adeline."

"I don't think you have to worry about that."

But he was worried. He knew he'd be worried all night about her falling asleep and sliding off the roof. Hard-on or not, he crawled around the cupola to where she was.

She had removed her black hoodie and was using it as a cushion for her back.

"Scoot up," he said.

"Why?"

He sighed. "Just for once, would you listen to me without fighting? I think you owe me a little trust."

She scooted up and he moved behind her. The hoodie did work well as a pillow. Once he was leaning against the cupola, he reached out and hooked an arm around Adeline's waist, pulling her back against him.

She stiffened. "What are you doing?"

"Making sure you don't fall asleep and fall to your death."

"I won't."

"Sorry, but I can't trust that. Now relax. The dragon promises not to devour you."

"Very funny."

He chuckled. "Oh, come on. Lighten up. You have to admit that it's kind of funny."

A moment later, a laugh escaped her. It was the first time he'd heard her laugh. She even laughed like a princess. The sound light and musical. Her body melted into his, and he realized too late that telling her to relax hadn't been a good idea. Now, he could feel almost the entire length of her body.

Her bare thighs conformed to his, her bottom

snugged into the vee of his straddled legs, and her soft breasts rested on his arms. It was like riding a horse double. He'd always loved riding double with a hot woman. And there was no doubt that Adeline was hot.

To keep his mind off the soft body he held, he tried to go back to their previous conversation. "So Hester Malone thinks I'm a dragon. She didn't mention that when I talked with her today."

"You talked with her?"

"She warned me about being vigilant." He paused. "I guess she had a point. I was nodding off when I heard you climbing the scaffolding. If you hadn't shown up, I'd probably be dead by now."

"So I saved your life." It was easy to hear the smugness in her voice.

"And I saved yours."

"Then I guess we're even."

"I guess we are."

She leaned her head back on his shoulder and he caught a whiff of herbal shampoo. "Although if I hadn't been on the scaffolding, they wouldn't have wanted to knock it down."

"I don't know about that. I don't think it was a spur of the moment plan."

She turned her head, her lips inches from his. "But why would they want to kill you?"

"Maybe whoever it is wants revenge on anyone involved with the ranch."

Thankfully, she turned away from him and took the sight of her tempting lips with her. "I should've known it wasn't you. You enjoy being a hero too much to be a villain."

A hero was the last thing Gage was. "I'm not a hero. I'm just a cowboy."

"That's what you want everyone to believe, but I think there's much more to your story than you're letting on. Why did you leave your family's ranch to work here? Don't you get along with your family?"

"I get along fine with them. But sometimes you need space to get your life back on track."

"How did your life get off track?"

He leaned his head back and looked at the stars. They seemed even brighter tonight. Maybe because he was still here to see them. His brush with death had made him a little philosophical.

"How does anyone get off track? It just happens. You take a wrong turn or a tragedy throws you off course. Before you know it, you're lost and can't find your way back."

Her silky hair brushed his chin as she nodded. "My family thinks I'm lost because of Danny. But the truth is, I've been lost for a long time. I've been so busy trying to make other people happy, I've forgotten to make myself happy."

"And what would make you happy?"

"That's just it. I don't know." She paused. "The one time I made a decision that I thought would make me happy, it ended up shattering other people's lives . . . and mine."

A drop of moisture hit Gage's hand. Followed by another. And another. It took a glance up at the clear sky before he realized Adeline was crying. He wanted her to regret breaking Danny's heart, and now that he had proof she did, it didn't make him feel any better. It broke his heart.

His arms tightened.

"Go to sleep, Adeline. I won't let you fall."

# Chapter Twelve

Adeline woke feeling . . . well rested. Since she hadn't woken up feeling well rested in almost a year, she was confused. Not just about feeling well rested, but also about the soft rumbling sound next to her ear and the bright light that seemed to be burning through her eyelids.

She slowly opened her eyes and squinted at the light. It took only a second to recognize the sun. Its bright rays just peeked over the horizon, offering a hug to the early morning sky. Adeline took a moment to enjoy the beauty before she realized the sun wasn't shining in her windows. There were no windows. There were no walls. Or a ceiling. She tried to sit up, but she couldn't move. She glanced down to see strong arms locked around her.

Everything came back in a rush.

She had set out to catch the dragon only to discover that the villain wasn't a villain after all. He was a hero just like everyone had said. He'd certainly saved Adeline. She'd be in a bent, crumpled heap like the scaffolding if not for Gage's quick thinking and reactions.

She shifted just enough in his arms so she could look at his face. He was sound asleep, his head tipped back against her black hoodie and his mouth slightly open and emitting a rumbling snore. She didn't know why his snoring made her smile. Maybe because it proved he wasn't as perfect as everyone thought.

But he was still pretty perfect.

With his long lashes resting on his high cheekbones and his strong jaw covered in sexy scruff and his mussed wheat-colored hair catching the first rays of golden sun, he looked like the kind of man any woman would feel lucky to wake up with.

Even if you were teetering on a rooftop.

A whistle drew her attention. She knew the whistle. It was Potts. He always went to the chicken coop early in the morning to collect eggs for breakfast. The chicken coop was right next to the barn. But if she yelled out for Potts, she would startle Gage and they might both go tumbling off the roof. So she lifted a hand and gently rested it on his face.

"Gage," she whispered.

His arms tightened, but he continued to sleep.

She couldn't stop herself from further exploring his face. She slid her palm over the bristle of his morning scruff, then placed her index finger in the dimple in his chin. She traced the fullness of his soft bottom lip, pressing the plump flesh and getting a peek of perfectly straight bottom teeth. Shamelessly, she didn't stop. She caressed each chiseled cheekbone and the delicate skin of his eyelids and the smooth flat plane of his forehead before she ran her fingers through the thick locks of his sun-kissed hair.

That's when his snoring stopped and his eyes slowly opened.

She should have pulled away.

She didn't.

"Good morning," she said in a voice that betrayed the quivery tingles in her tummy. The tingling grew even stronger when he answered in a sexy sleep-rough voice.

"Good mornin'."

She knew there was something else she needed to be telling him, but for the life of her, she couldn't think what it was. All words were lost in his heavy-lidded hazel eyes. Gage didn't seem to have words either. He just stared back at her. The tingles turned to a hot pool of need. She had spent so many years ignoring her needs. For her family. For Danny. But she didn't want to ignore her needs anymore.

Her fingers curled against his scalp, gripping his silky hair in her fists as she moved closer to his lips. She had just barely touched their softness when Potts started singing "Camp Town Ladies" at the top of his lungs.

Gage blinked and pulled away so quickly he banged his head on the cupola. He removed his arms from around her and cringed in pain as she shifted on the peak of the roof to face him.

"Are you okay?" She smiled. "I always seem to be causing you bumps on the head."

If the scowl was any indication, he didn't find her teasing amusing. "It's not my head. My arm muscles are cramped." He squeezed his eyes shut and gritted his teeth as he stretched his arms over his head. The sight of all those flexing muscles and the patches of dark blond hair beneath his arms had need pooling once again deep inside of Adeline.

"Here." She took one of his arms and rested his hand on her thigh, then started vigorously rubbing the muscles with both of her hands. When she glanced up, he was staring at her as if she'd gone mad. She understood his confusion. She had done a complete reversal. Last night, she'd been accusing him of horrible crimes. This morning, she'd tried to kiss him and was now massaging his muscles.

A blush heated her cheeks, and she stopped rubbing his arm. "Better?"

He continued to stare at her while Potts serenaded them with do-dahs. As those do-dahs started to fade, she realized Potts was heading back to the house and they would be stuck up there until someone else came along.

"Potts!" she yelled.

". . . oh, da doo dah day. Oh da doo dah—"

Gage put his fingers in his mouth and whistled so shrilly Adeline had to cover her ears. Potts stopped singing.

"Who's up there?"

"It me. Gage," Gage called down.

"What are you doing up there, boy?"

"It's a long story. Go get a ladder." He glanced

at Adeline. "And be discreet, Potts."

Adeline knew why he wanted Potts to be discreet. Gossip ran rampant on a ranch. If the gossips of Cursed got wind that Gage and Adeline had spent the night together on a barn roof, they'd be the talk of the town.

"Of course." Potts chuckled. "I can understand why you don't want anyone knowing you were fool enough to get stuck on the barn roof all night."

After Potts was gone to retrieve the ladder, there was an awkward silence. Mainly because Gage had gone back to staring at her as if she completely baffled him.

She stretched her arms over her head and bent from side to side. "Sleeping on a roof can sure tie you up in knots, can't it?" When he didn't reply, she searched for something else to fill the silence. "The new roof looks good. You and the ranch hands did a great job. I've never really been up here before. The view is breath—"

A ladder thumped against the edge of the roof cutting her off and Adeline sighed with relief. Her relief was short lived when she heard Wolfe's voice.

"I'm not letting you climb up on the roof of the barn, Potts. I'll get your damn chicken."

"I told you I can get it myself."

"And break your fool neck. I like your cookin' too much to let you do that."

"Stubborn Kingman!" Potts grumbled before he called up. "Sorry, Gage, but Wolfe caught me with the ladder on the way back from the shed."

"Gage?" Wolfe said. "What the hell is Gage doing up on the barn roof?"

"I would've found that out if you hadn't butted your nose in. Now I need to get back before my French toast casserole burns."

When he was gone, Wolfe laughed. "The boys in the bunkhouse are going to have a laughing fit when I tell them about this." The ladder jostled and creaked.

"Well, shit," Gage muttered under his breath before he shoved the hoodie at her. "Put this on."

She had just pulled it over her head when her brother's face appeared above the edge of the roof. The confusion in his eyes when he saw her was easy to read. As was his anger when the confusion faded.

"What the fuck is going on?"

She started to explain, but Gage cut her off. "You'll wait until we have your sister safely off this roof before I explain."

With the way Wolfe's eyes gleamed with anger, it didn't look like he was going to wait. But then he moved up the ladder and held out his hand. "Scoot down to me, Addie. Be careful."

She glanced at Gage once more before she scooted her way down the roof to where her brother waited. He helped her onto the ladder, then stayed close behind her until she was safely on the ground.

"Thank you, Wolfe," she said. "There's a reason I was up on the roof with Gage. The scaffolding—"

Before she could finish explaining, Gage

reached the ground and was greeted with her brother's fist.

"Wolfe!" She screamed as Gage's head snapped back. She hurried and placed herself between him and her brother. "What is the matter with you? I told you there was a reason I was on the roof with Gage."

"I'm not stupid, Addie. I've taken my share of women up to the barn roof to watch the sunrise." Wolfe pointed a finger at Gage. "I told you she was vulnerable and to stay away from her. Now pack up your things and get the hell off this ranch before I beat you to a pulp."

Adeline didn't know what made her angrier. That her brother hadn't given her a chance to explain or that he still thought she was some fragile doll he needed to protect. "Why you stupid, controlling ass!" She hauled off and punched Wolfe right in the mouth. It hurt her hand like hell, but it didn't seem to do anything to Wolfe.

Except make him stare at her in stunned surprise. "Controlling ass?"

"A stupid, controlling ass! You have no business telling anyone to stay away from me. I'm not some fragile piece of glass you need to protect. I'm a full-grown woman who can make her own decisions about who she wants to be with. If I want to be with Gage, I'll damn well be with Gage."

"He's not the right man for you, Addie. Believe me, I know his type. He'll only break your heart."

Before Adeline and Wolfe could continue their argument, Gage spoke.

"You don't have to worry, Wolfe. I'm not going to break Adeline's heart. I'm not interested in your sister."

Adeline didn't know why Gage's comment stung. She wasn't interested in him either. Okay, maybe she was a little interested. She couldn't deny she enjoyed kissing him. But it was just because she'd gone without kisses for so long . . . and because Gage was a great kisser. She certainly wasn't interested in starting something serious with him.

"Then explain what you were doing cuddled up on the barn roof," Wolfe said.

"Trying not to fall off," Adeline said. "We were stuck up there all night after stampeding cattle knocked over the scaffolding."

"What were you doing on the scaffolding with Gage in the first place?"

She hesitated for only a moment before she told the truth. "I was following him because I wanted to get evidence he was the one who has been causing all the trouble on the ranch. But after we were both almost killed by whoever is causing the trouble, I realized my mistake."

Wolfe's eyes narrowed. "Almost killed? But I thought you said cattle knocked down the scaffold—wait a minute, how did the cattle get out and why would they head straight for the scaffolding?"

"That's the million-dollar question," Gage said. "The only logical answer seems to be that someone was herding them."

Wolfe didn't look any happier, but his anger

was no longer directed at Gage. He released a long string of cuss words before punching the side of the barn with his fist. When he turned back to Adeline and Gage, he seemed more in control. "I guess I owe you an apology, Gage." When Adeline crossed her arms and glared at him, he reached out to ruffle her hair. "And you too, sis. You okay? You didn't get hurt, did you?"

"I'm fine. Thanks to Gage. If he hadn't reacted so quickly, I would've been a pile of broken bones."

Wolfe shot Gage a sheepish look. "Thanks, man. I bet you're pretty fed up with Kingmans not trusting you."

"You could say that," Gage said dryly. "Now if you'll excuse me, I'm going to go see if I can find any evidence of who is responsible for the cattle getting out." He nodded at Adeline. "Miss Kingman."

It was the same way he'd always addressed her. Especially when other people were around. But this morning, it annoyed her more than usual. Not because of their brush with death. Or because he had proven his heroism. Or because she had slept in his arms. She was annoyed because after sharing truths with each other last night, she no longer thought of him as Mr. Reardon, her employee. Or Mr. Reardon, a villain.

She thought of him as Gage, her friend.

She placed her hands on her hips and sent him an exasperated look. "After spending the night together, I think we're past proper last names. Wouldn't you say, Gage?" She waited for him to agree and use her given name. She should've known better.

"Whatever you say, ma'am." He turned and walked off.

As annoyed as she was, she couldn't help noticing how the dragon tattoo seemed to come alive with each flex of his back muscles.

"Are you sure Gage didn't try anything?"

Adeline turned to Wolfe. "Yes. But even if he had, it wouldn't be any of your business, little brother." She glanced down at his mouth, which was bleeding. Instead of feeling guilty, she felt a little cocky. "So behave or I'll give you another fat lip."

Wolfe touched his mouth and grimaced. "That's what I get for teaching you how to punch. Now I'm going to go help Gage look for evidence. When I find out who the guy is who keeps trying to kill my sister, he's going to wish he was dead."

Adeline didn't doubt it for a second. Which is why she intended to call the sheriff. Sheriff Dobbs might be inept, but he was the one who needed to deal with whoever was responsible. She wouldn't have her brother taking the law into his own hands and going to jail for good.

She searched for her cellphone and found it on the ground under the trees that surrounded the house, along with her pepper spray. Thank God she had dropped the canister or she probably would've sprayed Gage.

After she called the sheriff, she called the investigator Stetson had hired and told him what happened.

"So as you can see," she said. "I was completely wrong about Gage Reardon. He's not the one we're looking for."

"I figured as much when I discovered he was a decorated Marine."

Adeline halted in mid-stride on her way to the house. "A Marine? Gage was a Marine?"

"Not just any Marine. From the reports I read, the guy was a real hero."

Adeline wasn't surprised Gage was a hero, last night had certainly proven it to her, but she was surprised he'd never said a word about it. Although he hadn't said a word about his family owning a big ranch either. Gage liked to keep his secrets.

What other secrets was he keeping?

Adeline wanted to know. She wanted to know all about Gage. At one time, she'd wanted to use the information against him. Now, she just wanted to know the man behind the hero. The man who captivated her with his golden eyes and inflamed her with his kisses.

If she had to spend a lot more time with him to figure out the puzzle that was Gage Reardon, then so be it.

# Chapter Thirteen

As soon as Gage saw Stetson's number on the cracked screen of his cellphone, he knew that someone—probably Adeline—had called him and told him about what had happened. The hot shower and breakfast Gage had been looking forward to would have to wait a little longer.

"Hey, Boss."

"Why the hell didn't you call me?" Stetson snapped.

"I was planning to, but I've been a little busy with the sheriff." Gage glanced over to where Sheriff Dobbs and Tater were taping off the crime scene—and erasing any evidence by stepping on the tire threads the all-terrain vehicle had left in the mud. It was a good thing Gage and the investigator had taken pictures of the prints before the sheriff and deputy had gotten there.

"You should've called me before you called that idiot Dobbs," Stetson said.

"I didn't call Dobbs. Adeline did. She called the investigator you hired too." Gage still wasn't real happy that she'd done it without saying a word to anyone. Or that she'd called her brother and worried him over something he couldn't do anything about.

Stetson heaved a long sigh. "So Addie's really okay? When I talked to her, I could tell she was trying to make light of things."

"Adeline's fine." Last night, he'd discovered just how fine she was. But he had made a pact with his brain that he was not going to think about how nicely her body fit against his.

"Thanks to you," Stetson said. "She told me about how quickly you reacted. I'm indebted to you for saving her life."

"Just a gut reaction. No big deal."

"Still, I owe you. Especially when she told me that she thought you were the one responsible for everything happening on the ranch. I don't know where my sister would get such a crazy notion."

Gage wasn't sure why he defended her. "It wasn't so crazy. I do have full access and knowledge of the ranch. After what happened last night, the investigator and I both think it has to be someone who has both. It looks like whoever was herding the cattle was on a four-wheeler. Probably the four-wheeler we keep in the hay warehouse in the north pasture. After we saw the tread marks, I had some of the ranch hands check out all the ATVs we have. The one in the hay warehouse was the only one with fresh mud on the tires."

"Damn," Stetson said. "We leave the key in that one. Anyone could've used it. Did Sheriff Dobbs get prints off it?"

"No, but the investigator is doing it now. Although since the four-wheeler is used by all the ranch hands, he doesn't think it will help." A flash of red in the corner of his eye had him turning. Adeline was walking down the path that led from the house. She'd showered and changed into a plaid western shirt, cut off jean shorts, and bright red cowboy boots. Her hair was braided in the same long braid she'd worn the night before.

Like the night before, he had the strong urge to wrap the long rope of silky moonlight around his fist. Like last night, he ignored the craving. But he couldn't ignore the fact she was headed straight for him. She stopped in front of him and smiled.

"I guess that's my big brother you're talking to. I probably shouldn't have called him, but I knew he'd raise hell when he got home if we didn't." She took the phone from him. "Like I said before, Stet. I'm fine. The ranch is fine. And there's nothing you can do that's not already being done. So go enjoy your new bride and we'll see you in another week. Love ya." She hung up and handed Gage the phone back with an even brighter smile. "Sometimes you just have to cut my brothers off."

"A sister can get away with that. An employee can't." Gage slipped his phone into his front pocket.

"I think you're a lot more than an employee to my brother. Ever since you walked onto this ranch, he hasn't stopped singing your praises. As do all my other siblings." She sent him a sassy look. "I was the only holdout. Probably because, until the last few days, I hadn't spent a lot of time with you and gotten to witness your amazing ranching abilities."

"You don't need to brown nose me, Miss Kingman. I thought we'd figured out last night that we're even on the saving lives business."

"I thought we figured out this morning that we aren't going to use last names."

"I think it's best if we keep our relationship professional."

Her eyebrows lifted. "You call all my brothers and my little sister by their given names. Why don't you want to call me by mine? If you were any other man, I might think it was because you were interested in me. But you made it very clear this morning that you aren't. So what's the problem?"

The problem was that he'd lied through his teeth. He was interested in Adeline. Extremely interested. But he didn't want to be.

"Fine . . . Adeline."

She gave him another bright smile. "Thank you, Gage. Now go take a shower."

The abrupt subject change had him wanting to sniff his armpits. He hadn't realized he smelled so bad. He took a step back. "I intend to. Just as soon as the sheriff is through."

"Wolfe can stay with the sheriff. You need food. I heard your tummy rumbling last night. If you were hungry last night, I'm sure you're starving this morning. And put on a shirt." Her eyes lowered to his bare chest and he had to stifle the urge to shield himself from the heat of her gaze like a shy schoolgirl. "I wouldn't mind, but Potts has a thing about people sitting at his table properly dressed."

"Thank you, but I can eat in the bunkhouse."

"Last time I checked, they stop serving breakfast in the bunkhouse at eight o'clock. It's well after. Besides, you haven't lived until you've eaten Potts's French toast casserole."

He started to decline the offer again when his stomach chose that moment to loudly protest.

Once again, she blinded him with her smile. "I'll have Potts give you an extra helping." She waggled her fingers. "See you in a few." She walked away, and he couldn't keep his gaze from following her. She caught him in the act when halfway up the path she stopped and turned around. "And don't take too long or I'll have to come hunt you down." Her eyes twinkled. "If you remember, I have no problem barging into the bunkhouse."

The last thing he wanted to do was eat breakfast with Adeline. But with her threat and his stomach grumbling, he resigned himself to his fate. He didn't waste any time heading to the bunkhouse and showering. The last thing he wanted was Adeline to show up like she had last time. When he walked past the barn on his way to the house, he discovered the sheriff and deputy were gone and Wolfe was helping a couple ranch hands clean up the scaffolding.

"Dobbs and Tater had already made a mess of the area with their damn boots," Wolfe said. "So I figured I might as well get things cleaned up. Speaking of cleaning up. Where are you headed all dressed to kill?"

He probably shouldn't have put on his best western shirt and jeans. But it was too late now for regrets. "Your sister invited me to breakfast. I tried to say no, but she wasn't having it."

Wolfe grinned. "Addie doesn't take no for an answer when she's made up her mind about something. And we owe you more than just breakfast for saving her life."

"I would've done it for anyone."

Wolfe grew serious. "But you did it for my sister." He slapped him on the shoulder. "Well, what are we waiting for? Let's go eat. I'm starving."

Gage was relieved that he wouldn't be eating alone with Adeline. When he and Wolfe walked into the kitchen, Delaney and Buck were sitting at the table too. They had both been down to the barn earlier and knew what had happened, but Adeline seemed to have filled them in on more of the details.

As soon as Buck saw Gage, his grin almost split his face. "Well, if it isn't the dragon come to have breakfast with us." He held out his cup. "Can you reheat my coffee, Dragon? It's gotten a little cool."

Delaney socked his arm. "Don't you have any manners, Buck?" She pulled out the chair next to her and fluttered her eyelashes. "Come sit next to me, Gage. I don't mind a little extra heat."

"What are y'all talking about?" Wolfe asked as he took the chair at the head of the table. Gage went to take the chair Delaney had pulled out, but Potts blocked him.

"You sit over there by Addie, Gage. Del

shouldn't be rewarded for making fun of a guest." He tapped her on the head with his wooden spoon. "Mind your manners, young lady." He headed back to the kitchen leaving Gage to take the chair next to Adeline. She smiled sweetly at him before she answered Wolfe's question.

"Hester Malone was one of the reasons I was suspicious of Gage. She had a dream about a dragon causing all the problems on the ranch. And Gage happens to have a dragon tattoo."

"You're kidding!" Wolfe leaned his head back and roared with laughter. While Gage had found it just as funny, for some reason, he didn't care for Wolfe laughing at his sister.

"I heard the woman has correctly predicted more than a few things," he said dryly.

Wolfe sobered. "I'm not laughing at Addie for believing Hester. That woman does have some weird ability. I'm laughing at her thinking it was you just because you have a dragon tattoo. Lots of men have dragon tattoos, Addie. I even planned on getting one. But when the tattoo artist found out my name, he talked me into this one." He lifted his shirt to show off the snarling wolf on his pectoral muscle.

Potts whacked him hard on the arm with his spoon. "Watch your manners." He set down a casserole dish piled high with gooey chunks of cinnamon-and-syrup-covered bread. Gage's stomach rumbled again and he had to hold himself back from diving headfirst into the delicious-looking dish. Adeline must've heard his stomach because she grabbed the spoon just as

Buck was going for it and piled Gage's plate high.

"Geez," Buck said. "Leave some for the rest of us, Addie."

"There's plenty," Potts said. "I have another dish in the oven."

After the second dish was passed around and everyone's plate was filled, Gage would have started eating if Adeline hadn't taken his hand. He was struck a little speechless by the feel of her soft, warm fingers closing around his knuckles. He shot her a stunned look, but she only smiled.

"Grace."

All her siblings took hands. Buck held his out to Gage and grinned. "Try not to scorch me."

When they all bowed their heads, Adeline spoke in a soft, clear voice. "Dear heavenly Father, thank you for this meal we are about to partake of and all your many blessings." She hesitated. Her fingers tightened on Gage's hand. "And thank you for sending us Gage."

"And forgive Addie for thinking he was a dragon," Delaney added.

"Amen to that!" Buck said before he dove into his breakfast.

Gage quickly followed suit. Potts's French toast casserole was the thing that dreams were made of. Gage enjoyed every bite as he listened to the Kingmans chatter and rib each other. He had thought the meal would be awkward, especially after he and Adeline had spent the night together. But it wasn't awkward.

It felt like he was back at the Sagebrush Ranch with his family.

He ate three helpings of the casserole. Of course, Wolfe had four. Where the man put it, Gage didn't know. Delaney and Buck both ate two helpings. Adeline was the smallest eater with just one. But for some reason, Potts was extremely pleased by that.

"I see you finally got your appetite back," he said as he picked up her empty plate. He looked at Gage. "Maybe we need to have company more often."

Once breakfast was over, Gage thought he could finally escape Adeline. That wasn't the case. She followed him to the mudroom. He stopped at the back door and turned to her.

"I thought you weren't suspicious of me any more."

"I'm not."

"Then why are you following me?"

"I'm not following you. I'm going to check on Glory Boy." She took a straw cowboy hat off a hook and tugged it on.

Gage had intended to go check on the colt. With the accident and breakfast, he hadn't gotten a chance. But if Adeline was going, especially looking all Daisy Duke cute, he'd wait.

"Take Buck or Wolfe with you. After what happened, you can't be too careful."

"But I thought you'd be going to the stables."

He pulled on his cowboy hat. "I wanted to take a look at the all-terrain vehicle at the north warehouse."

"Then I guess I'll see you later."

Not if he could help it.

When Gage got to the warehouse, he headed to the all-terrain vehicle parked next to the huge rolled hay bales. He didn't know what he was looking for. If there was some evidence left behind, the investigator had probably already found it. Still, he wanted to make sure they weren't missing anything.

The mud on the tires was dried now. He pulled up the picture he'd taken of the tread marks. They were identical. He looked around the vehicle before checking out the entire area. The only thing he found was a Baby Ruth wrapper that had probably been left by one of the ranch hands. Or had blown there in the wind. Still, he carefully picked it up and folded it before putting it in the front pocket of his shirt.

When he didn't find anything else, he headed to his truck. On the way back to the ranch, he stopped off at the rundown house he was renovating for himself. While he was in the area, he figured he might as well do a little work on it. Anything to keep him away from the ranch and Adeline. A leak in the roof had damaged one wall of the living room. He had already repaired the roof and now just needed to repair the wall.

He spent the rest of the morning replacing the rotted two-by-fours. When he was sweeping up sawdust, he discovered a Baby Ruth wrapper. At first, he thought it had fallen out of his pocket. But when he checked, the first wrapper he'd found was still there. It was probably just a coincidence. Lots of people ate Baby Ruth candy bars. But the wrapper looked as new as the first one, and Stetson had told him that no one had lived in the house for years. So who had been there? And how had they gotten a key?

His cellphone rang, startling him out of his thoughts. He carefully folded the wrapper and placed it with the other one before pulling his phone from his other pocket and checking the caller ID.

He answered. "What's up, Buck?"

"You better get back here quick, Gage. Glory Boy is in a bad way."

# Chapter Fourteen

Adeline sat in the corner of the stall with Glory Boy's head on her lap. She stroked the foal's forehead and grew even more worried when he didn't even open his eyes. "Where is the veterinarian? It's been almost an hour since Buck talked to him."

"I don't know. He won't answer or return my calls." Gage sat on the other side of the foal, looking as concerned as Adeline. They'd moved Magnolia into another stall until they could figure out what was wrong with the foal. But the mare hadn't gone easily. As if sensing her son was seriously sick, she'd tried to pull free from Buck. She still whinnied pathetically.

Tears filled Adeline's eyes as she looked down at the lethargic foal. "I don't get it. He was doing so much better."

Gage shook his head. "I don't get it either. I talked with Tab. He hasn't let him out to pasture. All Glory's gotten to eat is his mother's milk. And no one, except me, your family, and Tab has been allowed near him since he's been sick. Which rules out someone poisoning him."

The thought hadn't entered Adeline's mind. "You think someone purposely poisoned Glory?"

"I thought it was a possibility. But after giving strict orders to Tab to keep everyone but family away from this stall, I don't see how they could have gotten to the foal. At night, the stables are locked tight."

Adeline glanced at the stall door and lowered her voice. "You don't think it could be Tab, do you? He does have full access to the ranch."

"Tab loves horses too much for him to poison one. And it would have been pretty difficult for him to hit himself in the back of the head and knock himself out cold." Gage glanced down at Glory Boy. "Maybe Glory being sick has nothing to do with what's been going on at the ranch. Maybe he's got some equine disease."

"But you don't think so."

He blew out his breath. "Not after last night. Whoever wants justice is becoming more ruthless." He looked at her. "Which means you and your siblings need to be more careful. I mean it, Adeline. Make sure you and Delaney don't go anywhere unless you're with Wolfe or Buck. Even then, you have to be watchful."

"And what about you?" She continued to stroke Glory's head. "You need to be careful too. I've been thinking a lot about the scaffolding accident. There's no way whoever it is could've known I was up there with you if he was busy cutting down fences and herding cows. He was after you. Probably because he knows you're watching all the time."

Gage snorted. "I haven't done that great of a job watching. Tab still got hurt. Lily got attacked. And you and Stetson were almost killed."

Adeline understood why her family had put so much trust and faith in Gage. He was the type of person who took it upon himself to save the world from injustices. When he couldn't, he blamed himself.

"You can't be everywhere at once, Gage. And I'm pretty sure a lot more things would be happening if you weren't watching over the ranch." She tipped her head to study him. "Why are you still here?"

"I thought we covered that last night."

"We did, but why the Kingman Ranch? There are plenty of other horse ranches in Texas."

Before he could answer, Delaney appeared at the stall door. She and Buck had been waiting for the veterinarian so they could show him to Glory's stall as quickly as possible. "The vet still hasn't shown up." She opened the gate and stepped in. "How's Glory doing?"

"Not well." Adeline stroked the foal's forehead. "We can't even get him to drink water."

Delaney studied the horse with sad eyes. "He was doing so well this morning when I checked on him. I even had him doing some tricks."

Adeline had watched her sister train horses. Delaney had always been able to get them to do just about anything with her love . . . and her homemade oat treats. The thought of the homemade treats had Adeline turning to her sister.

"Did you give Glory treats for his tricks, Del?"

"Yes. I gave him a couple." Delaney's eye widened when she realized what Adeline was getting at. "But I'm sure they didn't make him sick, Addie. I've given them to him before."

"Besides this morning, what other times have you given him the treats?" Gage asked. Delaney named off the times and Gage glanced over to Adeline. "They coincide with the times Glory has gotten sick."

Delaney shook her head. "Y'all know I would never poison a horse."

"Of course we know that," Adeline said. "But someone else could've tampered with the treats. Just like they tampered with Stetson's truck's brakes."

Gage got to his feet. "Where do you keep the treats, Del?"

"In the tack room."

There was no way to tell if the treats had been poisoned. But given that Glory Boy had been sickest after Delaney had given him the treats, it seemed likely. Delaney was devastated and left the stables in tears. Adeline would've gone after her if she hadn't been so busy trying to save Glory. The vet still hadn't arrived. Adeline didn't know if Glory Boy would last until he did show up. If they wanted to save the foal, they needed to do something now.

"I think we need to pump his stomach," she said.

Tab nodded. "I agree. We need to get that poison out of him."

She sent him a hopeful look. "Have you done

it before, Tab?"

Tab shook his head. "No, ma'am. I leave that to Doc Lovett."

Adeline looked at Gage, but he shook his head. Since she knew her siblings didn't have experience with pumping a horse's stomach that left only one person.

"Then I'll do it," she said. "I watched Doc do it a couple times."

Gage held up his hands. "Now, wait a second, Addie. I don't know if that's a good idea. I don't want you upset if something goes wrong. I say we wait for the vet."

"We can't wait, Gage. If we do, we could lose him."

Gage studied her for only second before he nodded. "Okay. What can I do?"

She gave him and Tab a list of items she'd need. While they were getting them, she ran back to the house to get one of her equine veterinary textbooks. She looked up the procedure and went over it, then looked it up on online to make sure nothing had changed since the textbook was published. After she felt semi-educated, she scrubbed her hands in the stable sink. Wolfe came in while she was doing it.

"How's Delaney doing?" she asked as she dried her hands.

"She's pretty upset. But Buck's with her." Wolfe smiled. "They might fight like cats and dogs, but if one of them is hurting, the other one is right there to comfort them." He lifted an eyebrow. "You sure you don't want to wait for the vet,

Addie?"

Adeline wasn't sure. In fact, she had started to have major doubts. What if she killed Glory rather than saving him? But before she could voice her fears, Gage stepped out of Glory's stall.

"Everything's ready."

Gathering her courage, Adeline nodded. Before she could head to the stall, Wolfe pulled her into his arms and gave her a tight hug.

"Good luck, sis."

Adeline needed all the luck she could get. She was a nervous wreck. Her hands shook so badly when she slid the tube in Glory's nose that Gage had to reach out and steady it. But once she saw that it didn't seem to cause the foal pain, she stopped shaking and did what needed to be done.

After they pumped the contents of the foal's stomach out, she knew she'd made the right decision. It was green and toxic looking. She continued to pump until the water came out clear. Next, she and Gage made up a charcoal slurry and pumped that through the tube to absorb any remaining poison. After that, they pumped in a laxative of mineral oil to coat the stomach and flush out the rest of the poison in the intestines.

She had just finished removing the stomach tube when the vet finally arrived. He was much younger than Doc Lovett and had kind brown eyes and a nice smile.

"I'm Doctor Michael Hanes," he said as he stepped into the stall. "Sorry I'm late. I had an emergency breech birth right when I was heading over here that I needed to see to first." He took in the situation, then looked at Gage. "You pumped his stomach?"

Gage smiled at Adeline. "Miss Kingman did. And she did a damn good job of it."

Adeline felt all flushed and happy. It wasn't just Gage's praise that made her feel that way. It was more the sense of accomplishment. She felt even happier when Dr. Hanes finished examining Glory Boy and what they'd flushed out of his stomach and agreed that it looked like a poisoning.

"You did the same thing I would've done, Miss Kingman. And extremely well. It looks like you've had some experience."

"A little."

"Well, you have a knack for it then. You want to help me get an IV set up?" He opened the bag he'd brought with him. "I think this little guy could use some fluids and some anti-inflammatories."

As they worked together to get Glory Boy set up on an IV, she and Dr. Hanes talked. Even though he had caused Adeline a lot of stress, he seemed like a nice man who was extremely complimentary about her skills at assisting him.

"You know I could use a good veterinary assistant," he said. "Would you be interested? If you're considering becoming a vet, it would be a step in the right direction. The best kind of learning is hands on."

"I'm sure it is."

Gage's dry comment had Adeline glancing up at him. A few minutes ago, he'd seemed as happy with their accomplishment as she was. Now he looked ticked off about something. His forehead was crinkled, his eyes narrowed, and his arms crossed over his wide chest. Obviously, he was still angry at the vet for not showing up sooner. But his anger faded when Dr. Hanes removed the IV and Glory Boy popped up on his gangly legs and trotted around as if he'd never been sick.

Tears of relief filled Adeline's eyes. Surprisingly, when she looked at Gage, she saw them in his eyes too.

He smiled at her.

She smiled back.

"I think he'll be fine," Dr. Hanes said as he packed up. "No solid food for a few days until his stomach heals. Call me if you need me."

"Thank you, Dr. Hanes," Adeline said.

"No problem. You did the hard part." Dr. Hanes smiled. "And please call me Michael."

"Call me Addie. I'll show you out."

Gage swung open the stall door. "I'll walk him out. After you, Doc."

After Gage left, Adeline and Tab cleaned up the stall. Tab took the buckets and tube to clean them while Adeline raked up the sour straw and spread some fresh. She was washing her hands at the big farm sink when Gage walked back in and joined her.

"I hope you were nice to Michael," she said as she took one of the hand towels stacked on the shelf over the sink. "He had a good excuse for being late."

He rolled up his sleeves in a jerky motion. "The

man needs to focus more on his job. Less on flirting."

"Flirting?" Adeline laughed. "Michael wasn't flirting."

He picked up the bar of soap on the edge of the sink and lathered his hands and halfway up his arms. There was something about lather on the hard, corded muscles of his forearms that made her feel a little lightheaded.

"If you didn't think that was flirting, Adeline. You need to get out more. The man was drooling all over you." He replaced the soap, then shoved his hands and forearms under the running water before turning off the spigot and giving them a shake. It turned out beaded water on muscles was just as appealing as soap. She had to resist the urge to slide her hand along his arms and collect the droplets. "Could I use that towel?"

Adeline pulled her gaze from his arms and handed him the towel. He briskly dried off. "I just think a vet should be more professional. I don't think you should have encouraged him."

"I did not encourage Michael!"

"Calling him by his first name is encouragement. So were all the smiles you gave him."

She placed her hands on her hips. "And just what business is it of yours if I want to smile at a man? Are you now the guardian of my virginity as well as my life?"

She realized what she had said as soon as the words were out of her mouth. Her face burned with embarrassment as Gage slowly turned to her.

"You're a virgin?"

She tried to lie, but lying had never been her strong suit. "Of course not. I mean . . . a woman my age . . ." She forced a laugh. "That would just be . . . weird. No. I've had sex." She told herself to leave it at that, but her mouth didn't listen. "A LOT of sex. In all different kinds of positions and with all kinds of . . . things."

Gage continued to stare at her. "Things?"

"You know, sexual . . . things. I've used them—" She cut off, realizing what a fool she was making of herself. "Fine! So I'm a virgin. Go ahead and laugh."

But Gage didn't laugh. His eyes only held confusion. "But how? I thought you and Danny planned to get married."

She swallowed. "Some people decide to wait until they're married before having sex. Danny and I were two of those people. It's not that strange."

But she could tell by the look on Gage's face that he thought it was strange. He started to say something, but Tab came out of the tack room. She could only pray he hadn't overheard their conversation.

"Y'all can go. I'll keep a close eye on Glory Boy tonight." Tab winked at Adeline. "You did good, Missy."

On the way back to the house, she couldn't help but think about the person who had poisoned Glory Boy. "Why would anyone want to kill a sweet animal that hasn't harmed a soul?"

"I don't know." He hesitated. "Do you know

of anyone on the ranch who likes Baby Ruths?"

The bizarre question had her glancing over at him. "The candy bar?"

He nodded. "I found some wrappers out at the north warehouse. And I thought that maybe you knew of a ranch hand who liked them."

"No. You think the person who left them could be the one who knocked down the scaffolding?"

"I don't know." He shook his head. "I'm probably grasping at straws. I just want to catch the S.O.B. so bad."

They arrived at the back door, and she turned to say goodbye. He'd removed his cowboy hat before they'd started working on Glory and his hair was endearingly messed. She reached up and smoothed back a strand. It was a simple gesture. At least that's what she told herself. At yet her heart beat even faster as the silky strand slipped through her fingers.

"Thanks for helping me with Glory Boy. I couldn't have done it without you."

He studied her. His hazel eyes gleamed like pure gold in the setting sun. "Why didn't you and Danny make love, Adeline?"

She should've known he wouldn't let it go. Gage wasn't a man who let things go. "I told you. We wanted to wait until we were married."

"We? Or just you? Because I'll bet money that Danny didn't want to wait to have sex with you. Have you looked in the mirror? Any man in his right mind would want to have sex with you. Hell, the damn vet just met you and he wants to."

"Well, I'm not like that. I don't have sex just for

the sake of having sex. I have to love the person first." She realized what she'd said the second the words were out of her mouth.

Gage didn't look at all surprised by her revelation. "So you didn't love Danny."

She had held the secret for so long. Too long. She realized if she could trust anyone with it, she could trust Gage.

"I loved Danny. I just didn't love him like that. I wanted to love him like that." Tears filled her eyes. "I tried . . . I really tried. I loved him in every other way. He was my best friend and my confidant and my comforter when both my parents passed. I thought passion would come with time—once I stopped grieving for my father. And once I wasn't so stressed about making sure Wolfe, Delaney, and Buck got off to college. And once the ranch was doing okay. But then all those things happened and I still . . ."

"Didn't desire him," Gage finished the sentence for her.

She looked away and nodded.

"So why didn't you just tell him?"

A tear trickled down her cheek. "I did. And that's why he died."

# Chapter Fifteen

THE MATTRESS IN the bunkhouse was much softer than the hard scaffolding platform, but Gage still couldn't sleep. All night his mind kept wandering back to his conversation with Adeline. He'd been right. Adeline had just been stringing Danny along and making him believe she cared about him more than she did.

But Gage had also been wrong.

He'd thought Adeline had hurt Danny because she was a selfish princess who thought of no one but herself. But that wasn't the case. Adeline wasn't selfish as much as selfless.

After Elizabeth Kingman had died, Adeline had taken on her mother's role. She'd run the Kingman castle and helped raise her younger siblings. When she'd finally escaped to college to follow her own dream, her father had died. Once again, she'd put her own needs on hold and returned to the ranch to help Stetson and her entire family deal with their grief.

But Gage had to wonder if she'd ever taken the time to deal with her own. No wonder she struggled with figuring out her feelings for

Danny. Grief sent your emotions into a tailspin. Gage knew that first hand. He had lost so many comrades in arms. Each time, he'd felt sad and angry and confused. After Danny's death, Adeline had been an easy target to get rid of some of that suppressed anger. He'd become obsessed with her. He'd Googled her and the Kingman family and read everything he could get his hands about them. There hadn't been much about Adeline. But there had been plenty about the Kingman Ranch.

Once he'd left the military and come back to the States for good, he'd been unable to let his obsession go. When he met Adeline, she fit perfectly into the mold of the old, heartless heartbreaker he'd convinced himself she was. But he'd been wrong.

Adeline wasn't heartless. If anything, she had too much heart. She cared about her family. She cared about animals. And she had cared about Danny. Which is why she'd struggled to tell him that she didn't want to marry him. Why she blamed herself for his death.

But she wasn't to blame. Danny being heartbroken hadn't caused his death. If anyone was to blame, it was Gage. If he had just talked to their commanding officer and kept Danny from going out on the night patrol, he might've been able to save him.

Giving up on sleep, Gage got up and got dressed. Outside, the stars were as brilliant as the night before and the moon was even fuller. He patrolled the area around the stables and barn, and then moved to the house. All the lights were off. Even Adeline's. But he had to wonder if she slept. Or if she was lying there thinking about Danny.

Gage should've stopped her when she'd turned to go into the house. He should've stopped her and told her that it wasn't her fault. Instead, he'd just stood there like an idiot and watched her disappear inside. Probably because if he'd told her it wasn't her fault, he'd have to tell her who he was and why he'd come to the Kingman Ranch. He didn't want her hating him.

Not when he'd started to feel anything but hate for her.

Which meant it was time to leave. There were too many reasons why falling for Adeline was a bad idea. She was Stetson's sister. Gage's boss. Danny's girlfriend. Not to mention the fact that Gage wasn't boyfriend material. Not when he was still screwed up from Iraq.

As soon as they caught whoever was causing the problems at the ranch, Gage needed to turn in his resignation. Until then, he was going to stay away from Adeline Kingman.

He turned from the house and headed for the garden. He shined his flashlight into the trees and around all the flowers and shrubs before he checked to make sure the cottage doors were locked. The cottage was where Lily had grown up with her parents who had been the Kingmans' gardeners. Now, it was where Lily and Stetson lived.

After making sure the doors were secure, Gage

headed to the stables to check on Glory Boy. On the way, he passed the hedge labyrinth. When he first arrived at the ranch, he'd gotten lost in the maze for a good hour before he'd found his way out. Now he knew the maze better and couldn't resist the challenge. Near the center of the labyrinth, the soothing splash of water drew him into the secret garden. He stepped through the hidden break in the hedge. The scene that greeted him took his breath away.

A beautiful princess slept on the stone ledge of the fountain, covered in a light blue comforter.

He should be angry Adeline was out here alone. But it wasn't anger that welled up inside of him at just the sight of her. It was a feeling he couldn't describe. The same feeling he'd gotten whenever he looked at the picture Danny kept over his bunk. No matter what Gage had told himself just moments earlier, he couldn't seem to stay away.

She drew him like the warm glow of a campfire on a cold, moonless night. He moved closer until he was standing over her. She slept with her hands on her stomach and her hair spilling around her in pale waves that reflected the moonlight. Her cheeks were flushed and her light lashes rested against the soft shadows beneath her eyes.

In those lashes, tears glistened.

Gage's heart tightened. He was responsible for those tears. He never should've goaded her about her relationship with Danny. A strong need to make amends for his actions filled him. He knelt next to her and bent his head, kissing the tears from each lid.

She inhaled sharply, and her eyes fluttered open. "Gage."

The one word held relief and something more. Something that made him feel like he wasn't broken.

Cradling her face in his hand, he kissed her flushed cheek and the tip of her perfect nose and the curve of her jaw and the slope of her throat. Then he kissed his way along the soft skin of her neck to the spot behind her ear. He pressed his lips there and breathed in her scent. A scent that was solely Adeline. A mixture of everything pure and good.

He should stop. But he couldn't. Especially when her cool hand settled on his neck, her fingers burrowing through his hair to press him closer.

Needing to taste her, he sucked her sweet skin between his lips. She tasted as pure as she smelled. He sucked harder. She moaned and arched her hips. He knew her need. He felt it in every fiber of his being. As he kissed his way to her lips, that need grew and consumed him.

They had kissed two times before, but there was some component in this kiss that had been missing from the other two. Something that turned the heat Gage had felt before to a blazing inferno.

He didn't just burn for Adeline.

He incinerated.

The soft slide of her lips and wet heat of her mouth as she surrendered to the kiss undid him. Any resolve he had to stay away from her turned to ashes at his boots. He wanted her. He wanted all of her. He wanted to erase all thoughts of Danny and claim her as his own.

But just thinking Danny's name had him breaking the kiss. He sat back against the edge of the fountain and closed his eyes, trying to regain any semblance of composer.

"Why did you stop?" she asked in a soft whisper.

He took off his hat and ran his fingers through his hair. "Getting involved with you is too complicated, Addie."

"Because of my brother?"

"That . . . and other things."

She sat up. "What other things? Do you have a girlfriend back home? Was she the one in the family picture I saw on your website? The one with her arm around you?"

"No, I don't have a girlfriend back home. That's my sister, Katie."

"Then what?"

He needed to tell her the truth. She deserved that. He took a deep breath and released it. "I was a Marine."

"I know. The investigator told me. He said you were a decorated hero."

He tipped his head back on the fountain ledge and looked up at the sky. "A hero. I've yet to figure out how taking lives makes you a hero."

"Maybe because taking those lives saved many more lives." Her cool fingers slid over his forehead in a soothing way that had the tension in his shoulders easing and his eyes sliding closed. "Maybe being a hero is just trying to keep the people you care about safe."

A lump rose to his throat. "I couldn't even do that." He hadn't kept Danny safe. And he should have. He pulled away from Adeline and sat up. "What I'm trying to tell you is that you don't want a screwed-up guy like me, Addie. You want someone like Michael Hanes. Someone who doesn't have all the baggage I do. Someone who can give you the happily-ever-after you deserve."

He expected her to take his rejection with her usual calm demeanor. He did not expect her to get pissed.

She jumped up from the fountain with her eyes flashing. "All my life I've been surrounded by men who thought they knew me. My daddy thought I was his sweet little princess. Stetson thinks I'm a housekeeper and Wolfe, Buck, and Delaney's babysitter. Buck and Wolfe think I'm their innocent virginal sister. And Danny thought I was his hometown sweetheart. Because I loved them, I wanted to please them and be all those things. I was so busy being what other people wanted me to be, I stopped being what I wanted to be." She glared at him. "And I'm tired of trying to fulfill the images the men in my life have of me. That includes you. You don't know me. You don't know what I need. If you don't want to kiss me, then don't kiss me. But don't put your hang ups on me."

He got to his feet. "That's not what I was doing. I want to kiss you—I want to do a lot more than kiss you. But I don't deserve you."

She clenched her fists. "That's such bullshit!"

This new feisty side of Adeline was kind of scaring him . . . and turning him on. Although that probably had more to do with the nightgown she was wearing. The thin material clung to every line of her stunning body, including the breasts she pressed her hand to.

"Do you think I don't have my fair share of baggage, Gage? Everyone does. And I'm not asking for forever. I just want some naughty, get-down-and-dirty sex. So do you want to or not?"

He stared at her in stunned shock. "Are you drunk?"

She crossed her arms over the sweet swells of her breasts that he was having a hard time keeping his gaze from. Especially after her offer. "Perfectly sober. In fact, I'm thinking straighter than I have in a long time. I've waited my entire life to feel desire for a man. And don't say you don't desire me. Kisses don't lie. We ignite when we kiss and you know it."

He did know it. Even talking about sex with Adeline had him as hard as the stone fountain. "I desire you, Addie. But you are a virgin, and I'm not. Not by a long shot."

"Good. I'd hate to have my first time be with someone who doesn't know what he's doing." She slipped off her nightgown, exposing a body that crumbled all his defenses like a grenade.

# Chapter Sixteen

As the seconds ticked by and Gage refused to say a word, Adeline started to wonder if she'd misread everything. Maybe Gage didn't desire her. Maybe the heat of their kisses had all been one-sided.

Her side.

Embarrassment washed through her like a wave. The one time she had gone after what she wanted, it had completely backfired in her face. Now there was nothing left to do but pull together her shattered pride and . . . get the hell out of there.

She lifted her chin and forced a smile. "I guess I misread things." She bent to pick up her nightgown, but before her fingers could even close around the soft cotton, Gage was on his feet taking it from her hand. His gaze wandered over her body in a slow slide that had her heart bumping against her ribs. "You didn't misread anything. I want you. I want you more than I've ever wanted a woman in my life. But you're so damn beautiful that I'm afraid to touch you."

His words caused her desire to deepen into

a warm glow. "Touch me, Gage," she breathed. "Please touch me."

He slowly lifted his hand and reached out to cover her breast. The warmth of his palm against the chilled peak of her nipple had her inhaling sharply. She held her breath as he gently squeezed and lifted. He shifted his hand and his callused thumb gently brushed her nipple, causing it to contract and send a shower of sparks through her body.

Finally, here were the fireworks she'd been missing all her life. She burned for him, and only him, with a white hot flame that consumed her. As he caressed her breast and teased her nipple, he slipped his other hand around her waist and pulled her closer, his lips finding hers in a wet, devouring kiss.

There was something so erotic about being naked in a man's arms when he was fully dressed. When he stopped fondling her breast and slid both his hands to her butt cheeks to tug her closer, the feel of his clothing against her bare skin had the sparks of desire burning even brighter.

The soft cotton of his shirt teased her sensitive nipples. The rough denim of his jeans sent tingles up and down her legs But it was his rigid fly prodding her stomach that left Adeline feeling lightheaded and weak-kneed. If she could just get that hard knot a little lower . . . or get the quivering need between her legs a little higher.

She stood on her tiptoes, but she was still short by a few inches. As if sensing her need, Gage palmed her butt cheeks and lifted her, pressing her needy center to his hard desire.

Adeline couldn't describe the sensation that rocketed through her. She moaned and wrapped her legs around his hips, rubbing against his hardness in the way that gave her the most pleasure. She had almost reached orgasm when Gage stopped kissing her.

"Slow down, Adeline, or you're going to have me going off like a green kid."

"But I want . . ." She rubbed against him faster.

"Shit . . . stop, Addie." He unhooked her legs. When her feet were firmly back on the ground, he kissed her again. "I know what you want, baby. And I'm going to give it to you. I'm going to give it to you good."

Okay, maybe she could wait.

He released her and grabbed the comforter off the ledge. He carried it over to the grass lawn next to the fountain. Once he had it spread out, he came back and scooped her into his arms and carried her over to lay her down. After a quick kiss, he sat down on the ledge of the fountain and tugged off his boots.

She had to admit it felt deliciously sensual to be lying completely naked beneath the wide starry sky while a hot cowboy undressed in front of her.

"Take it slow," she said.

Gage stopped tugging off his socks and glanced at her with confusion. She blushed, but she had waited too long for this to not ask for what she wanted.

"Take it slow removing your clothes," she clarified.

His confusion cleared, and he smiled a sexy smile as he dropped his socks to the ground. "Yes, ma'am."

He stood and slowly unbuckled his belt, slipping it inch by inch out of the loops. When it was free, he ran the long piece of leather through his fingers before doubling it over and snapping it. Why the sound of leather hitting leather would make her squirm with need, she didn't know. But it did.

"Hmm?" He hummed deep in his throat. "So the princess likes it a little rough."

She hadn't ever thought she'd like it rough, but if the feeling of disappointment that assailed her when he dropped the belt was any indication, she must.

As if reading her thoughts, he smiled wickedly. "Another time, baby. I promise." He pulled out the tails of his western shirt from his waistband, then slowly popped open each snap. One by one, until he'd revealed a slice of dark golden chest hair, muscled ribs, and finally a hard ripped stomach.

With bated breath, Adeline watched as he slowly slipped the shirt off his shoulders. She had seen him without his shirt before. Slept snuggled against those hard muscles. But his masculine beauty still had her pulse picking up ... especially the pulse between her legs. It throbbed even more when he reached for the button of his fly.

He took his time slipping the button out of the hole, then inched down his zipper. White cotton bulged out through the opening. Adeline couldn't help but feel lightheaded from the proof of his desire for her. When his jeans were off and he stood before her in nothing but snug-fitting boxer briefs, there was little doubt of it. The cotton of his underwear barely restrained his hard length.

Slowly, he pushed his elastic waistband down. Adeline lost all the moisture in her mouth. Living on a horse ranch, she had seen a lot of studs in her day. But none like this stud.

He stood for a long moment, letting her look her fill before he asked, "So what do you think, Miss Kingman. Will I do?"

Not waiting to act like an inexperienced virgin, she gave him a thorough onceover. "Quite nicely."

He moved toward her with a grace surprising for a man his size. She expected him to get on top of her. Instead, he stretched out beside her. He kissed her, his lips moving slowly and thoroughly on hers, as his hand slipped down to caress the throbbing spot between her legs.

His fingers seemed to know exactly how to pleasure her. They stroked and teased. Caressed and invaded. Until every muscle trembled with the need for release. When she came, it was like no orgasm Adeline had ever given herself. It was intense and explosive and Gage drew it out until she gasped his name and grabbed his hand.

But he still wasn't done with her. Before the last shiver of contentment had washed over her, he trailed kisses down her body.

"What are you..." she started, but then quickly

shut her mouth as his hot, wet mouth touched her still quivering center. Within seconds, she was tumbling back into an amazing orgasm.

She was nothing more than a liquid puddle of satisfaction when he moved over her and entered her. There was a twinge of pain, but only a twinge, followed by the full stretch of Gage being deep inside of her. He gave her time to adjust before he started to move. Slowly. Deeply.

There were no fireworks like she'd experienced earlier. The feeling that washed over her was more like embers after the fire is out. The flames of desire had burned hot, but the feelings that grew as Gage made love to her held a warmth that flames couldn't sustain. There was a connection that had nothing to do with the physical act. As she started to move and met each thrust, the connection grew. She didn't desire release. She didn't want to be released from this feeling. She wanted it to go on forever.

Too soon, his pace grew faster and his muscles tightened. But before he could reach orgasm, he pulled from her and finished with his hand.

At first, she was confused. Then she was grateful.

"Thank you," she said when he had settled next to her. "I was so busy getting what I wanted, I didn't even think of contraception."

"You shouldn't thank me, Adeline. I should've waited until I had a condom. The pull out method is not exactly the most reliable."

The thought of having a baby with Gage should've concerned her. Instead, it made her feel giddy. But she kept that piece of information to herself and cuddled closer to his body and smiled.

"Well, I am grateful. That was awesome."

His arms tightened around her, and he kissed the top of her head. "I couldn't agree more. But we probably better get up and get dressed before someone stumbles upon us—like your brothers."

"So what if they do? My brothers don't have any right to tell me how to live my life. If I want to have sex with my ranch manager in the garden maze, I'm going to."

He chuckled and lifted a strand of her hair, running his fingers through it. "Why do you come to the maze when you're upset?"

Great sex must act like a truth serum. Or maybe it was the soothing way he stroked her hair. Either way, she found herself answering honestly. "I guess it's just habit. When I was younger, I came here when I was upset because I thought the fountain had magical powers and could grant my wishes. But I've given up on wishes. They always seem to backfire on me."

"How so?"

"I wished that my parents would stop fighting and my mother died. I wished that my father would stop fooling around and he died. And finally I wished for some way to break it off with Danny . . . " She let the sentence trail off. "My wishes seem to be cursed."

"You weren't responsible for Danny."

"I know." She did know that now. But it didn't ease her grief. "But I wish I had loved him enough."

Gage stopped caressing her hair. "You can't help who you fall in love with."

"Have you been in love?"

He didn't answer. And that was answer enough. Not wanting to think about the woman he'd fallen in love with, she turned in his arms and smiled up at him.

"Tell me about your family."

He seemed more than happy to change the subject. "Very similar to yours. We fight and bicker, but love each other deeply."

"And your parents?"

"My mama fell in love with my daddy when they were in second grade. According to him, she pestered him for years until he finally give in." Adeline laughed. She wished her parents had had that kind of love. "Then there's my Nana," Gage continued. "She's a force to be reckoned with. She's feisty just like you."

Feisty wasn't a word she'd thought people would ever use to describe her. She had to admit she kind of liked it. And since she was being feisty . . .

She leaned up and kissed him deeply before she drew back and smiled. "Wanna do it again?" She knew he wasn't opposed to the idea when she felt him harden against her.

But the stubborn man still argued.

"No, Addie. I'm not having sex with you again without contraception."

"Lucky for you, I think I know where to find some." She gave him a quick kiss on his startled mouth before she got to her feet. "Come on."

Gage got up. "Stop, Adeline. We're not having sex again. You need to get back to the house before someone notices you're gone and gets worried."

"No one is going to notice that I'm gone. And if they do, I don't care. I've spent years worrying about my siblings. They can worry about me for one night."

He sent her a beseeching look. "Adeline, please go back to the house."

There was a time when she would've gone along with a plea issued by someone she cared about. But now she realized that sometimes you had to put your own needs first. From the looks of Gage's erection, he had some needs too. He was just too stubborn to admit it.

She looped her arms around his neck and gave him a hot, thorough kiss. When she had him groaning and rubbing his hard-on against her, she drew back and smiled. "Okay. If that's how you want to play it, you go on back to the bunkhouse and spend the rest of the night thinking about what you could be doing to my body in a nice comfortable bed in the cottage." She reached down and fisted him in her hand. "And what I could be doing to yours." After a few strokes that had his eyes glazed over, she released him, scooped up her nightgown and blanket, and slipped through the opening in the hedge.

She grinned as she heard him cussing a blue streak. She could just imagine his inner devil struggling with his inner hero. By the time she reached the end of the labyrinth and he hadn't shown up, she figured the hero had won. She was about to head back to the fountain to yell at him when he came hustling around the corner of the hedge in his underwear and cowboy hat, his arms filled with his clothes and boots.

Adeline had to bite back her laughter. "Change your mind?"

His gaze swept her still naked body. "You're enjoying driving me crazy, aren't you?"

She sent him a sweet smile. "Very much."

He hesitated for only a second before he smiled. "Then lead the way, Adeline Kingman. I'm all yours."

Something splintered inside her heart at his words. Maybe because she knew he wasn't all hers. One day he would leave the Kingman Ranch and go back to his family. Maybe even to the girl he loved. But for tonight, Adeline planned to pretend he was all hers.

She turned and headed toward the garden cottage. "Then come on, cowboy. Let's see what kind of stamina you've got."

# Chapter Seventeen

Peaceful sleep had eluded Gage for so long that he'd forgotten what it felt like. There had been no nightmares. No regrets or guilt. There had just been sweet oblivion. And he knew exactly who was responsible.

He rolled to his side and looked at the woman next to him. Last night, she'd looked like a princess out of a storybook sleeping on the fountain. This morning, she looked like a real woman. Her hair was a wild, tangled mess, her jaw was slack, and a little bit of drool hung on the corner of her mouth.

Gage much preferred this real woman to the princess.

Last night had been the best night of his life. He had always thought that experience made for better sex. But Adeline had taught him that emotions did. She'd taught him the difference between having sex and making love. He and Adeline had made love. She had pulled feelings out of him he had never felt with another woman. And never would. It was time he accepted the fact that he was in love with her and probably had been in love with her since he'd first seen her picture and listened to all Danny's stories.

Now the question was: where did he go from here?

After last night, he couldn't leave her. No matter how much he thought she'd be better off without him and all his baggage. But if he wanted any kind of relationship with Adeline, he had to tell her the whole truth. His parents had taught him that you couldn't base a good relationship on lies. But if he told her the truth, she might not ever be able to forgive him.

It was between a rock and a hard place. Live with the guilt of his lies. Or live without Adeline.

Living without Adeline was something he didn't think he could do.

He pulled her closer and buried his nose in her sweet-scented hair. She sighed with contentment and burrowed into him, issuing a soft yawn that stirred the hair on his chest.

"What time is it?"

"Time for us to get up and get you back to the house before anyone finds out you're missing." He glanced at the sun shining in through the window. "Although it's probably too late for that."

She made a sexy humming sound deep in her throat. "Mmm, don't worry. I'll just say I got up early to check on Glory Boy."

"In your nightgown?"

She giggled. He loved the sound of her laughter. "That would put a kink in my alibi. Not that I need an alibi. My family is used to me hiding out in my tower room. Which should give us plenty of time to . . ." She brushed her tongue over his nipple and a spear of heat shot straight to his groin. Now he was the one humming.

"Mmm, stop, Addie. You might not need to get up, but I really need to—" He cut off when she nipped his nipple with her teeth. He went from semi-hard to rock solid in seconds. She continued to torture him with licks and nips as she moved down his body. When she reached his straining hard-on, she gave it one brief kiss on the moist tip before she sat up. Her hair fell around her bare shoulders, playing peek-a-boo with her full breasts, and her eyes were heavy-lidded and sparkled with desire and mischief.

"Well . . . I guess we should go then." She started to get up, but he growled low in his throat and pulled her down to the mattress, rolling on top of her.

"I think I can spare a few more minutes."

The sun moving up in the sky ceased to exist as they made slow, unhurried love. When they were both breathless and satisfied, he scooped her up in his arms and carried her into the shower where they explored each other's bodies some more. Adeline seemed infatuated with every part of him. But especially his tattoo. It felt like heaven to have her soft, soapy hands running over his back.

"Why a dragon?" she asked as her fingers skated down the dragon's tail that curved around Gage's left buttock.

He tried to keep his mind on the question, but

it wasn't easy when she was driving him crazy. "I like dragons."

"You like horses too. Why not a horse?"

"Horse tattoos aren't as badass to a cocky eighteen-year-old who wants to impress girls. Although if you look closely, you'll see that my dragon isn't all that badass."

Her fingers paused, and he could just picture her standing on her tiptoes to get a better look of the dragon's head. She must've figured it out because she started laughing. Not a little chuckle, but an out-and-out laugh. He turned and tried to send her an annoyed look. But he was too happy to be annoyed.

"It's not that funny."

"Oh, yes it is," she gasped. "Big badass Gage has a tattoo of the dragon from the cartoon Shrek—pretty eyelashes and all."

Her laughter was contagious, and he joined in. "I didn't realize it until one of my buddies pointed it out. If I ever see that tattoo artist again, I'm going to kick his ass. He knew exactly what he was doing."

Adeline bit back her laughter and slid a soapy hand along his waist and around to his butt cheek. "Now don't be too mad at him. I happen to like men with tattoos of cartoon dragons." She slid her other hand slowly down the muscles of his stomach. "Want to see how much?"

They didn't get out of the shower until the water had turned ice cold. Shivering and laughing, they toweled each other off. When his stomach growled loudly, Adeline smiled. "The dragon sounds hungry. I'll see if I can find something to make for breakfast,"

"You cook?"

She sent him an annoyed look. "Yes, the princess cooks. And I'll be happy to prove it."

"I would love to try your cooking, darlin', but I really need to get to work."

"You're not going anywhere. As your boss, I'm giving you the day off." Before he could argue, she sailed out of the bathroom. He smiled and shook his head as he went into the bedroom to search for his underwear. He found them under the bed. After he pulled them on, he headed to the kitchen to collect the clothes he'd dropped there the night before. When he got there, he found her wearing his western shirt and pulling a box of pancake mix from a cupboard. She looked thoroughly disappointed when he reached for his jeans.

"I kinda like what you have on."

He laughed. "I like what you have on too, but I need to do some work today." As he picked up his jeans, his wallet fell out of his pocket. It bounced a few times on the floor before it fell open at Adeline's bare feet. The photograph in the clear plastic ID holder had him making a dive for the wallet. Before he could grab it, Adeline picked it up. Her brow knitted and her lips parted in surprise. When she lifted her gaze to him, her blue eyes were filled with stunned confusion.

"Where did you get this picture of me?"

He moved closer. It broke his heart that she stepped back. "I can explain, Addie."

"Answer the question, Gage? Where did you get this?"

He tried to find words that wouldn't hurt her. But the truth hurt. "I got it from Danny."

"You knew Danny?"

He nodded. "I served with him in Iraq."

She shook her head. "But I don't understand. If you knew Danny and you had this picture of me ... then you knew who I was. But you never said anything. Why didn't you say anything?"

"Because I didn't want you to know who I was. I didn't come here to work for Stetson. I came here because of you. Because I wanted to meet the woman who had broken my best friend's heart."

Adeline's eyes welled with tears, and Gage had never hated himself so much. "No wonder I thought you hated me. You did. Hester was right. You came here for revenge."

He wanted to deny it, but he couldn't continue to lie to her. "I was angry after I came back from Iraq. I needed an outlet for that anger. So yes, I did blame you for Danny's death and I wanted you to pay some kind of price—even if it was just giving you a piece of my mind."

"So why didn't you?"

He ran a hand through his hair. "I don't know. Maybe I wanted to hold onto my anger. Because when I focused all my anger on you, I didn't think about the lives I had taken or how I should've watched out for Danny that night." He looked at her. "But I was wrong, Addie. You're not to blame."

Her eyes filled with tears, and his heart cracked wide open. "Yes, I am. I'm to blame for not being strong enough to tell Danny the truth sooner. I should've told him long before he went to Iraq. Instead, I tried to be what he wanted me to be. That's what I've done all my life. I've let people I care about tell me what I'm going to do, instead of deciding for myself. I'm to blame for not being strong enough to make my own choices. Regardless of how those choices hurt others. But I'm through keeping my true feelings inside. I want you to leave, Gage. I want you to leave now."

"No, Addie. Please don't make me go. Last night was . . ." He tried to come up with the words to tell her what last night had meant to him. What she meant to him. But before he could find the words, the door opened and Stetson and Lily stepped in. There was no time to grab his jeans and put them on. All Gage could do was stand there in his underwear and let Stetson come to his own conclusions.

Which didn't take long.

Stetson's gaze swept over Gage and then went to his sister. If her wearing his shirt wasn't incriminating enough, the tears running down her cheeks were.

Stetson dropped the suitcases he carried and, in three strides, was across the room. "You sonofabitch!"

Gage braced for the punch, but it didn't help. Stetson's fist hurt like hell when it connected with his jaw.

"Stetson!" Lily yelled as Gage stumbled back

into a chair and knocked it over. "Stop it. Stop it right now."

But Stetson didn't listen as he punched Gage again and again. "I asked you to watch out for my family and you seduced my sister! I trusted you like a brother and you betrayed me."

Gage figured he would've beaten him to a pulp—and Gage would've let him—if Adeline hadn't started hitting her brother over the head with a broom. Gage was as surprised as Stetson was. Especially after he'd hurt her so badly and deserved to get his butt kicked.

"Oww!" Stetson turned to Adeline. "What are you doing?"

"I'm trying to knock some sense into that thick skull of yours. This is none of your business so quit butting your nose in where it doesn't belong."

"It's my business when my family gets hurt. And from those tears on your face, I'd say that Gage hurt you."

Adeline swiped at her cheeks. "You can't keep me from getting hurt, Stet. Sorry, but that's just not how life works. And what makes you think Gage seduced me?"

"Don't even try to tell me that you seduced him. You're too sweet and innocent."

"Maybe that's my problem. Maybe being sweet and innocent doesn't get you anything in life but regrets. I'm tired of regretting things. I'm also tired of you thinking you're in charge of my life. I came back from college because I didn't want you to lose the ranch. But that doesn't mean you're my boss, Stet. I own just as much of the ranch as you do. And I've worked just as hard for it. If I want to have a one-night stand with a ranch hand, you won't say a word or butt your nose in where it doesn't belong. I'm a big girl. I can take care of myself."

Gage was proud as hell of Adeline for standing up for herself, but he could've done without the "one-night stand with a ranch hand" part. Even though he knew it was just her hurt talking, it still stung.

"Adeline is right, Stet," Lily said. "I know you've helped raise your siblings and you feel more like their father than their brother. But you aren't their father and you need to start treating them as equals instead of kids you have to take care of. I agreed to cut our honeymoon short because you were so worried after Addie called. Being worried about your siblings getting injured or killed is one thing. Being worried about them getting emotional hurt is another. They're adults, Stetson. They are going to have their fair share of heartache." She hooked her arm through his and gave him a kiss on the cheek. "Now, come on, honey. Let's let Gage and Adeline finish their discussion in private."

Adeline moved toward the door. "We're finished."

Gage went to stop her, but her icy look halted him in his tracks. He held up his hands. "Just give me a few minutes to explain, Addie."

"You've had over a year to explain, Gage. I think that's plenty of time." She picked up the wallet that was sitting on the table and pulled out the picture. Then she walked out the door with her head held high.

Gage started to go after her, not caring that he was still in his underwear, but Stetson stopped him.

"I might not have any say in Adeline's life. But I still have a say in who works on this ranch. You've got an hour to get your things and get off my property. And if I ever see your face around here again, I'll shoot first and ask questions later."

# Chapter Eighteen

When Adeline left the cottage, she hoped she could sneak upstairs to her room without running into anyone. She needed time to think. Time to absorb what she'd found out about Gage. But as her luck would have it, everyone was in the kitchen when she came in the back door. Delaney and Buck were sitting at the counter laughing as they watched Gretchen and Wolfe having some kind of tug-of-war with the shirt Wolfe was wearing.

"Please give me your shirt, Mr. Kingman," Gretchen tried to pull his shirt up. "Coffee stains. I'd feel just absolutely horrible if I ruined your shirt with my clumsiness. You have to let me get this in a presoak right away."

"Leave me be, woman!" Wolfe roared and tugged his shirt back down.

Delaney suddenly noticed Adeline standing there. "Addie?"

Buck stopped laughing and Wolfe and Gretchen stopped their shirt battle and turned to her. She must have been a sight because everyone's eyes widened.

"What happened to you?" Buck asked. "Why are you running around in a man's shirt? And why do you look like you've been crying?"

Wolfe didn't need Adeline to answer. Probably because he had seen more than his fair share of heartsick women. He growled low in his throat. "I told Gage to stay away from you. Now I'm going to have to kill him."

"Gage?" Buck stared at her. "You and Gage?"

"Good for you, sis!" Delaney punched the air. "It's about time one of us got a little action." She sighed. "Although I was hoping it would be me that Gage rolled in the hay."

"TMI!" Buck yelled as he covered his ears. "You want me to puke up my breakfast burrito, Del?" He lowered his hands and looked at Adeline. "Was it really Gage who made you cry, Addie? He doesn't seem like that kind of guy."

Adeline hadn't thought so either. But if he'd lied about why he'd come there, what else had he lied about? "You don't know Gage," she said. "None of us do."

"I know enough to kick his ass." Wolfe started for the door, but Adeline stepped in front of him.

"You are not going to kick his ass, Wolfe."

"But he hurt you, Addie."

She couldn't argue the point. She was hurt . . . but mostly angry.

He'd lied to all of them. But especially to her. Still, she couldn't let Wolfe beat him up. Stetson had already taken care of that. Gage hadn't lifted a finger to stop him. Probably because he knew he deserved it.

"Don't act like you haven't hurt your fair share of woman, Wolfe," Delaney said. "If you'd been beaten up every time, you'd be punch drunk."

"She's right," Adeline agreed. "You can't keep me from getting hurt, Wolfe. I'll get over it. Now if you'll excuse me, I need to get dressed." She turned and headed for the stairs.

Once in her room, she sat down on the bed and looked at the picture she still held in her hand. She remembered Danny taking it the night of their senior prom. She had been dancing with her friends and was all hot and sweaty . . . and slightly drunk. Danny had called her name, and she had turned to see him holding the digital camera he'd brought with him. He had snapped the picture and then put the camera in the pocket of his tuxedo jacket. She had forgotten all about it until now.

The photo was worn, like it had been handled often. She had to wonder if it had been by Danny. Or Gage. Or maybe both. Why had Gage kept the photograph? And right in the front of his wallet where he would see it every time he opened it? He said that he'd been obsessed with her. She didn't want to be any man's obsession—a princess put up on a pedestal to admire but not touch. Her father, brothers, and Danny had treated her like that. Like a fragile ornament to be displayed and protected, but never treated like a person.

She wanted a partner. Someone she could share everything with. And someone who could share everything with her. Gage had said himself that he had a lot of baggage. Did he mean he had more secrets? Could she have a relationship with a man she didn't completely know or trust?

A tap drew her attention to the door. Gretchen peeked her head in. "Can I come in?" When Adeline nodded, she stepped into the room and held up a container of ice cream. "I brought my mama's cure for lovesickness. Since my mama has spent most her life lovesick, we went through a lot ice cream. Which could explain my weight problem." She sat down on the bed and pulled the lid off the ice cream and handed Adeline one of the two spoons she carried. After they'd each eaten a few bites, she asked. "Do you want to talk about it?"

Adeline took another bite of chocolate ice cream before she released some of her anger. "Gage is a big, fat liar."

"Most men are." Gretchen licked the back of her spoon. "My mama says it has to do with fear."

"Fear?"

Gretchen nodded. "Men lie to women because they fear we'll find out what idiots they are and leave them. Mama was an expert at seeing through a man's lies and leaving him. What idiotic thing did Gage do?"

Adeline told her friend the entire story. When she was done, Gretchen had tears in her eyes and both hands clutched to her chest. "Oh, Sweet Lord, that is the most romantic thing I've ever heard."

"Romantic? He came here to get revenge."

Gretchen shook her head. "I don't think so. I think he was a hero hurting from losing his friend.

It sounds to me like both of you loved Danny and were struggling with guilt—you because you broke up with Danny and Gage because he couldn't save him. That's what grief does. It twists things around and makes you feel angry and sad and confused. It's hard to accept that it was just Danny's time and nothing anyone could've done would've changed that."

Gretchen smiled sadly. "Forgive yourself, Addie. And forgive Gage. If he had told you who he was to begin with, your brothers would've kicked him off the ranch and you would still be hiding in your tower."

"But before we made love, he should've told me."

"True." Gretchen's eyes twinkled. "But I'm sure you can think of some naughty ways to make him pay for lying. You shouldn't make yourself suffer too by breaking it off with a man who could be your Mr. Right just because he did something stupid."

Adeline left her spoon in the container and leaned back on the pillows. "But what if he's not my Mr. Right? There was a time I thought Danny and I were perfect for each other. I've proven that I'm not exactly good at understanding my own feelings."

Setting the container of ice cream on the nightstand, Gretchen turned to her. "Then maybe you need to spend more time with Gage to figure things out. But you certainly can't figure them out by sitting here eating ice cream with me." She leaned over and took Adeline's hands. "Like my mama always says, 'The best way to deal with any problem is to talk it out.' Go talk to Gage, Addie. Give him a chance to explain."

It only took a moment to realize Gretchen was right. She was tired of hiding in her tower with a broken heart. Tired of being the fragile Kingman princess who everyone needed to protect. It was one thing to tell people you were a grown woman who made your own decisions and another to start acting like it.

She smiled at her friend. "Your mama must be a wise woman to have such a wise daughter. I hope I get to meet her one day."

A strange look entered Gretchen's eyes. "Umm ... well, she's kinda a home body so I don't know if that will ever happen. But let's not talk about my mama now. You need to get dressed and go find Gage."

Getting dressed would've gone much quicker if Gretchen hadn't vetoed four of the outfits Adeline chose before she okayed a yellow sundress that showed more skin than it covered. When they got downstairs, Adeline discovered her entire family gathered in the kitchen.

"I can't believe you beat him up and fired him, Stet?" Delaney said. "No wonder no cowboy will look cross-eyed at me."

Adeline stepped into the kitchen. "You fired, Gage? How could you, Stetson? You had no business—"

Stetson held up his hands and cut her off. "I've already gotten bawled out, Addie." He glanced at his wife. "And I realize that I overreacted."

"I don't think kicking his ass and firing him was overeating." Wolfe's gray eyes glittered with anger.

"Because you happen to be an extremely volatile man," Gretchen said. "Who needs to simmer down . . . and take off that shirt so I can try to get the stain out of it. Of course, it's probably too late. It looks dried in." She went to touch the coffee stain on the front of Wolfe shirt, but he sent her a warning look.

"Leave me be, woman."

Before Gretchen could reply, Delaney piped up. "I don't see what the big deal is about Adeline choosing Gage as a lover. Has anyone looked at the man? He's hotter than a deep fried jalapeno pepper."

Buck groaned. "I swear Daddy should've whooped up on you more when you were a kid, Del. Unlike you, Addie is not just looking for sex. If she chose Gage, she must really like him." He looked at Adeline. "Do you, Addie?"

She nodded.

"And how does he feel about you?" Stetson asked.

"I don't know. But I plan to find out." She took out her cellphone. But Gage didn't answer her call. And Adeline couldn't really blame him. He had given his all to protect the family and all he'd gotten in return was beaten up and fired. She hadn't even given him a chance to explain before she'd walked out on him. Which meant she needed to be the one to take the next step.

"I'm going to the Sagebrush Ranch," she said.

"The Sagebrush Ranch?" Wolfe said. "Why would you go there?"

"That's Gage's family's ranch," Stetson said.

Wolfe stared at him in disbelief. "You didn't think you needed to share that information with the rest of us?"

"Gage asked me not to. He didn't want you treating him differently just because his family owns one of the biggest ranches in Texas."

"Damn," Delaney said. "Cute and a wealthy rancher. Way to go, Addie! You need to go after that man fast. And if he has single brothers, I'll be happy to come with you."

"I'll go with her," Wolfe said.

Adeline was about to set her siblings straight when Lily spoke up. "She doesn't need any of us tagging along. This is something Addie needs to do alone."

Stetson pointed a finger at Adeline. "I expect you to check in often so I know you're okay. And don't stop along the way."

Adeline gave him a kiss on the cheek. "I'll call you when I get there."

She felt so confident that she was making the right decision when she was with her family. But when she got up to her bedroom and she and Gretchen were packing, she started to have doubts.

"What if I get there and he's not happy to see me? Or what if I get there and discover that another secret he's been keeping is a girlfriend?"

Gretchen zipped Adeline's suitcase closed. "Or what if you get there and you two work everything out and live happily ever after?"

"Oh, Gretchen." Adeline hugged her tightly. "I'm so happy I found you."

"I'm happy too." Gretchen drew back with tears in her eyes. "I didn't have a lot of friends growing up. We moved a lot and I weighed a few pounds more than I do now and I talked too much to compensate for my insecurities about being the new kid on the block. Although I'm still pretty overweight and talk too much."

"You're not overweight. You're perfect. And you only say things that need to be said."

Gretchen smiled. "You're a good person, Addie Kingman. Now go get that man of yours."

Adeline still had doubts, but once she left the Kingman Ranch, a feeling of excitement tingled in her stomach. It was the first time she'd taken a road trip by herself since college. There was something freeing about leaving all the responsibilities of her family and the ranch behind. When she got to Cursed, she pulled into the gas station to fill up so she wouldn't have to stop again. While she was there, she decided to run in and get some snacks for the road. She hadn't eaten and was starving. She was surprised to find her cousin Jasper sitting behind the counter.

"Hey, Jasper. You weren't busy enough at Nasty's?" she teased.

He laughed. "I stopped by for gas, and Dalhart asked me to cover for him while he ran to Good Eats and picked up his to-go order." He finished off the candy bar he was eating and tossed the wrapper in the trashcan. "How's it going, cuz? I heard about the scaffolding accident. That sounds like a close call. I'm glad you're okay."

Adeline wasn't surprised that news of the accident had gotten around. Especially to Jasper, who spent so much time on the ranch. But she was surprised he knew she'd been on the scaffolding with Gage. The only people who knew were her family. They wouldn't have said anything. They didn't want gossip to get around about her and Gage spending the night on the barn roof together.

"Who told you I was with Gage?" she asked.

Jasper took a long time answering. Finally, he smiled slyly. "I wouldn't want to get anyone in trouble for gossiping. So what can I get you, cuz?"

The entire time she picked out her snacks she couldn't shake the feeling that whoever had talked to Jasper could very well have been the one who caused the stampede. As Jasper rang up her canned iced tea and snacks, she couldn't help pushing him for an answer.

"You need to tell me who told you about me being on the scaffolding with Gage, Jasper," she said as she handed him her credit card. "It's important. It might help us figure out who the demented maniac is that's causing all the trouble."

Jasper had turned to run her credit card. He froze and her card slipped from his fingers and landed on the floor. "Demented maniac?"

"What would you call someone who mutilates animals and tries to kill people all in the name of justice? He can't be sane."

"Maybe he thinks he has just cause." He bent

over to pick up the card.

She started to say there was no just cause for what the man had done when Jasper's t-shirt sleeve rode up on his arm as he reached for her card. Her cousin had a tattoo. Below the edge of his sleeve she could just make out the wings and flaming nostrils.

She sucked in her breath sharply. Jasper stood and turned to her.

"What's a matter, cuz? You look like you've seen a ghost." The smile he sent her wasn't his usual friendly grin. It was evil and . . . terrifying. "Or maybe just a demented maniac."

# Chapter Nineteen

IT HADN'T TAKEN Gage long to pack. He hadn't brought a lot with him to the Kingman Ranch and he was leaving with even less.

Namely his heart.

As he drove away from the ranch, his chest felt as hollow as a fifty-gallon drum. In his rearview mirror, he watched as the castle grew smaller and smaller. Adeline's tower was the last thing he saw as he turned onto the road leading away from the ranch. He had to wonder if she was watching him leave. Were her eyes filled with tears or hate?

He couldn't stand the thought of her crying, but he would prefer tears to her hatred. Even if he deserved her hate. He had certainly screwed things up. He didn't have a clue how to go about fixing them. Especially when her brothers wouldn't let him anywhere near her.

His phone rang and, in his hurry to pulled it out of his shirt pocket, it slipped from his fingers and fell into the crack between the seats. He pulled off the road and parked his truck to search for it. He was thoroughly disappointed when he pulled the phone out and discovered it wasn't Adeline who had called. It was his grandma. He called her back and just hearing her grumpy voice made him feel better.

"Well, it's about damn time that you returned my calls," she snapped when he answered.

"Sorry, Nana. I've been a little busy."

"You still trying to track down that villain?"

"Actually, I haven't been working on that much." He paused for only a second before he spilled his guts. "I met a girl, Nana."

A relieved huff of air came through the receiver. "Well, hallelujah, thank you, Lord. I've been wearing out my bad knees praying for this moment. It's about time the good Lord paid attention and saw fit to give you your soul mate."

"I wouldn't get too excited about your prayers being answered just yet." Gage ran a hand over his face, cringing when he touched the bruises Stetson had inflicted. "I might've totally screwed up the Lord's plans."

"So fix it." Leave it to his grandmother to get straight to the point.

"That might be easier said than done."

"Psssh! Who said life was easy? Me and your papa started the Sagebrush Ranch with nothing but three scrawny cows and not a clue of how to run a cattle ranch. Talk about screwing up. We made more mistakes in the first few years than probably any rancher in the history of cattle ranching. But we refused to give up. We learned from those mistakes and kept on fighting for what we wanted. And I expect nothing less from my grandson. Now is this gal worth fighting for or not?"

There was no doubt about it. "She's worth fighting for."

"Then what's stopping you from getting her?"

"Her three angry brothers."

"Only three?"

Gage laughed. "Okay, Nana. I'll fight for my girl."

"You do that. And don't call back unless you're on your way to Sagebrush with that little gal in tow. Do you hear me?"

"Yes, ma'am."

After he hung up, Gage turned his truck around and headed back to the ranch. With his jaw and eye throbbing, he decided a covert mission was the way to go. There were only three ways to get to Adeline's room. The front door. The back door. And the window. There was only one option that would get him past Adeline's bodyguards.

After parking at the bunkhouse, he changed out of his cowboy boots and into his running shoes. Not wanting his phone to alert anyone of his mission, he left it in his truck. He'd done a lot of rock climbing with his Marine buddies over the years. But that had been with security harnesses and ropes. Scaling a wall with no safety measures was a little scarier. But he kept his mind focused and his eyes on his next foot or hand hold.

It took him a while. When he reached Adeline's balcony, he swung a leg over the railing. He heard a squeal and almost lost his footing. He grabbed onto the rail and pulled himself onto the balcony. Gretchen stood there holding a container of ice cream and a dripping spoon.

"Mr. Reardon! What are you doing here?"

"I'm here to see Adeline."

Gretchen moved over to the railing and glanced down before she looked back at him with stunned eyes. "You climbed the castle wall?" She held the hand with the spoon to her chest, dripping chocolate ice cream onto the front of her apron. "That is about the most romantic thing I've ever witnessed in my life. I knew you loved her." Her eyes turned sad. "It's too bad she's not here to see it."

"She's not here? Where is she?"

"She's on her way to Sagebrush Ranch to find you."

The hollowness in his chest filled with joy and a mad thumping. "She left the ranch and is driving all the way to Sagebrush to see me?"

Gretchen smiled. "She wanted to prove her love for you just like you wanted to prove your love for her." She sighed. "It just makes me want to tear up, it's such a perfect love story. But it won't turn out perfect if we don't get you two together. You have to call her and stop her."

"I don't have my phone."

"Shoot, I forgot to charge mine last night." She grabbed his arm and pulled him inside. "We'll just have to use one of the Kingmans'."

Gage had no intentions of confronting the Kingman brothers, especially when he'd snuck into Adeline's room. "I think it's best if we skip telling the Kingmans I was here. I'll call Adeline after I get back down. Or better yet, I'll catch her on the road."

Gretchen clung to his arm. "I can't let you climb down. If you plummet to your death, Adeline will never forgive me. And I'll never forgive myself. I'll create a diversion so you can sneak out the front door."

Gretchen's idea of a diversion was screaming "Fire! Fire!" at the top of her lungs. Gage stood behind Adeline's door listening as all the Kingmans came running up the stairs. He waited for Gretchen to direct them down the opposite hallway before he slipped out the door. Unfortunately, not every family member had listened to Gretchen's cry for help. He ran into Wolfe sitting at the kitchen counter eating. When he saw Gage, his eyes narrowed and he dropped his fork to his plate.

Gage held up his hands. "I don't want to fight you, Wolfe. I just came to find Adeline."

"Why?"

Gage could've gone into all the details, but he decided to keep it simple. "I love her."

"For how long? For your entire life or only until you get sick of her in bed?"

After thinking he might lose her forever, he didn't even pause before answering. "I want to spend the rest of my life loving her. If she'll have me."

Wolfe studied him for a long minute. "If you're lying, they'll be no place you can hide." His eyes grew confused as he sniffed. "Do you smell smoke?" Just as he said it, the fire alarm went off. He jumped up and ran from the room and Gage was right on his heels. By the time they got to

Wolfe's room, Buck and Stetson had the fire put out, but there was a huge hole burned in the middle of Wolfe's mattress.

Wolfe turned to Gretchen. "You set my bed on fire?"

She swallowed hard and shook her head. "I swear it was an accident. I was burning a piece of paper to create a little smoke and a cinder kinda got on your bed and ... well, it does give a whole new meaning to burning up the sheets."

Wolfe growled low in his throat. Before he could take his anger out on Gretchen, Gage stepped in. "It's my fault. Gretchen was trying to create a diversion so I could get out of the house without causing another scene."

"How did you get into the house?" Lily asked.

"He scaled the tower wall just like a prince." Gretchen sighed.

"No shit? You climbed the tower?" Buck looked thoroughly impressed. "That's awesome. You need to teach me how to do that."

Delaney snorted. "You're no prince. You're a frog who will break your fool neck."

Before the siblings could get into it, Gage spoke up. "I know y'all probably have a lot of questions about what's going on between me and Adeline." He looked at Stetson. "And I'm sorry I didn't tell you about my feelings for her sooner, but I was a little confused myself."

Stetson nodded. "I apologize for losing my temper. You're not just an employee, Gage, you're my friend and I should've given you a chance to explain."

"I have a lot to explain, but first I need to talk to Adeline and stop her from traveling all the way to Sagebrush Ranch." Before he could ask to use one of their phones, five cellphones were being held out to him. He smiled his thanks and took Stetson's.

But Adeline didn't answer.

"She's probably proving a point," Stetson said as he took his phone back. "She was pretty adamant about me treating her like a my kid sister instead of a grown woman. I bet she'll answer if you call her from your phone."

But Adeline didn't answer when Gage called her. He started to get more than a little worried.

"Maybe her phone just went dead," Buck said.

Wolfe shook his head. "After the crash, I made sure she has a phone charger in her car. And she's probably using her phone's GPS to get to Sagebrush. I don't have a good feeling about this. I should've gone with her."

Gage's gut was telling him something wasn't right too. "I'm going to head out and see if maybe she had car trouble or stopped in Cursed."

"I'll go with you," Stetson said. "I'll keep trying to call her while you drive." He looked at his siblings. "Y'all stay here in case she comes back to the ranch." He kissed Lily. "Call the sheriff and tell him to keep a lookout for Adeline's car."

On the way into Cursed, Gage and Stetson didn't talk much. Stetson kept trying to call Adeline and Gage tried not to panic. When they got to town and didn't spot her SUV, Stetson pointed at the Malone's house.

"Maybe she stopped to talk to Mystic and she'll know something."

Gage pulled in and parked. Before they could make it to the porch, the screen door flew open and Hester stepped out. "It's about time you got here. The dragon has risen. I just saw his evil face in my tea leaves."

Mystic followed behind her grandmother. "Hessy, please don't start. I'm sure Stetson and Gage didn't stop by to hear about what you saw in your tea leaves this morning."

"We're here to see if you've seen Addie," Stetson said.

Mystic shook her head. "No, I haven't seen her. Why? Is she okay?"

"Hell, no, she's not okay!" Hester snapped. "That's what I'm trying to tell you. The dragon's got her."

Gage stared at her. "I thought I was the dragon."

Hester looked thoroughly exasperated. "Didn't you pay attention to what I told you the other day? You're not the dragon. You're the warrior."

"Then who's the dragon?"

"His face isn't clear, but he's someone close to the family. And he has Adeline."

"Where? He has her where?"

Closing her eyes, Hester started rubbing the purple crystal that hung around her neck and breathing deeply.

"Hessy—" Mystic started.

Hester opened her eyes and pointed a finger at her granddaughter. "No talkin'!"

Mystic rolled her eyes, but stayed quiet as Hester went back to her crystal rubbing and deep breathing. "It's some kind of a house with building materials in it. And I see a wrapper. A Baby Ruth wrapper."

"Oh, for goodness sakes, Hessy. The dragon likes candy bars?"

Before Hester could answer, Gage turned and headed back to his truck.

"Wait a minute, Gage." Stetson followed after him. "Where are you going?"

"To fight a dragon and get my girl."

# Chapter Twenty

Adeline should have been scared. She was trussed up like Thanksgiving turkey and watching a man pour gasoline all around her. But she wasn't scared. She was pissed.

Jasper was the one who had killed the old bull, Sergeant, and set fire to the barn. Knocked Tab out and attacked Lily. Tampered with Stetson's truck brakes and stampeded the cattle into the scaffolding. All while acting like a smiling, good-natured, trusted member of the family.

Which explained why she hadn't reacted quickly enough. When she saw the dragon tattoo, she should have run. Instead, she'd stood there stunned while Jasper reached over the counter and grabbed her. She'd fought him, but he'd easily gotten her down to the floor and gagged her with his bandana, then secured her hands and feet with the duct tape Dalhart conveniently sold at the gas station. Adeline had prayed that Dalhart would return or someone else would show up, but no one had. Jasper was able to leave her trussed up on the floor while he'd pulled her SUV into one of the garage bays, then he'd placed her in the back seat and driven away.

She thought he would take her to some remote place to kill her. Instead, he'd brought her back to Kingman Ranch and the old foreman's house. It made sense now. If she died on the ranch, everyone would assume she was murdered by the same person who had done everything else.

Just like before, no one would suspect Jasper. No one would think a Kingman would want revenge on his own family. Jasper had gotten away with everything else. He'd get away with murdering her.

"You just had to figure it out, didn't you, Addie?" Jasper shook out the last of the gas on the pile of lumber in the corner. "You just had to piss me off by calling me a demented maniac." He dropped the can and shook his head. "I'm not a demented maniac. I just want justice. Justice for everything your family has taken from mine. You got it all. The huge ranch, the castle on the hill, more money than you would ever need. What do I have? I work in a rundown bar that my grumpy grandfather expects me to work like a dog for." He walked over and bent to get right in her face. "Do you think that's fair, Addie? Do you think that's right?"

Since she was gagged, she couldn't reply. All she could do was glare back at him.

He laughed. "So the sweet little princess finally found the Kingman courage." His smile faded, and he sighed. "I was never after you, you know? I didn't expect you to be in Stetson's truck or on the scaffolding. Of course, to begin with, I wasn't really after anyone. I just wanted to take out some of my frustrations. So I killed that old bull, set fire to the barn, poisoned those treats Delaney makes for her horses. But when I got away with all those things, a plan started to form. What if there was a way I could get the ranch? Stetson was the only one standing in my way. Wolfe doesn't give a shit about it. And you, Delaney, and Buck wouldn't be able to handle it on your own. You would've happily handed over the reins to your favorite cousin." Jasper's eyes got a crazy look in them. "But then Stetson had to hand over control to Gage while he was gone. And I started to worry that you and your siblings would trust him to handle things on the ranch more than you would trust me. Gage isn't the type of man who would let me take over—family or not."

He was right about Gage. But completely wrong about Adeline and her siblings. Wolfe might act like he didn't care about the ranch, but he did. So did Delaney and Buck and Adeline. If something had happened to Stetson and Gage, she and all her siblings would've stepped up to make sure the ranch survived. Jasper would have never run it.

"Well, I hate to bring a close to this interesting conversation, but it's time for me to go, cuz." He reached out and smoothed a strand of hair off her forehead. "You are so beautiful. I always thought we'd make good kissing cousins." She recoiled at the thought, and he laughed. "No? Well, it's probably for the best. I'd hate to have to kiss and kill." He straightened and pulled a lighter from his pocket.

Now Adeline *was* scared. Fear rose up in her as he flicked the lighter to life. The first image that popped into her head was of Gage. She had been having doubts about the validity of her feelings. Doubts about whether or not Gage was the right man for her. But she didn't have any doubts now. Suddenly, everything was crystal clear. Hester had once told her that she would marry a warrior. She had always thought Hester had been talking about Danny. But Gage was her warrior. He was the type of man she could count on to always be there for her. He'd gotten her over her fear of the stables. Saved her from the falling scaffolding. Stood by her side while they'd cared for Glory Boy. And helped her trust in herself and her emotions.

She trusted her emotions now.

She loved Gage.

He had made some mistakes, but so had she. She hadn't told Danny that she didn't love him enough to marry him and now she hadn't told Gage that she did love him enough.

It looked like she would never get the chance.

"Sorry, Addie," Jasper said. "But, if it's any consolation, you're heaven bound. I, on the other hand, am headed straight for—"

The sound of truck tires on gravel cut him off. He let the lighter go out and hurried to the window.

"Shit. It looks like the cavalry has come to save their princess. And maybe fate is finally with me and I can take out three birds with one stone."

He winked at Adeline before he grabbed a two-by-four from a stack in the corner and moved to stand against the wall by the front door.

A second later, the door burst open. Adeline tried to scream a warning, but it came out muffled as Gage and Stetson charged in the door. Jasper hit Stetson in the back of the head with the board. Adeline gave another muffled scream as her brother fell to the floor. Then Jasper swung at Gage. But Gage dodged at the last second and deflected the board with his arm, knocking it out of Jasper's hands. Jasper rushed over to the pile of wood in the corner. Gage charged after him, but froze when Jasper flicked the lighter back to life.

"You don't get the ranch, you sonofabitch. I'll die before a damned drifter takes what is rightfully mine." Jasper touched the flame to the gasoline-drenched wood and it immediately ignited into a ball of fire.

Gage went for him, but Jasper grabbed a hammer from the toolbox and swung. Gage ducked and came at him again, backing Jasper toward Adeline. She wanted to strike out at him. But being tied to the chair, all she could do was sit there and watch . . . unless she could figure out some way to move the chair and trip Jasper. She waited until he was close before she pressed her bound feet against the floor and pushed. The chair toppled backwards. She hit the floor with a jarring impact, but it worked. Jasper tripped over her and Gage dove on him.

Through the haze of smoke, she couldn't see what was happening. But a few seconds later,

Gage was at her side, cutting the tape from her hands and feet with a pocket knife before he carried her out the door. They were both coughing from the smoke. He set her on the ground a few yards away and took the bandana from her mouth, then he tied it around his face and ran back inside the house.

Seconds later, he returned with his arm around Stetson. Adeline was relieved to see her brother walking on his own. But her relief faded when Gage released Stetson and turned back toward the house. Before he could reach the doorway, there was an explosion and glass broke and flames shot out the windows.

After only a moment's hesitation, Gage started for the door again.

"Gage!" she screamed as she stumbled to her feet. The entire house was now engulfed in flames. There was no way Gage could go inside and survive. But he would try. She knew her man. Thank God, he hesitated long enough for her to reach him and throw her arms around his waist.

He jerked off his bandana and gasped for air. "Let—me—go. I—can—save—Jasper."

She held him tighter. "No you can't. But I can save you."

They heard the crack of splintering wood and watched as the roof of the house caved in.

Stetson must've called 911 and then the ranch because only a few moments later, Buck's big green monster truck showed up with Buck, Lily, Delaney, and Wolfe. Then came the fire truck, ambulance, and ranch hands. It wasn't shocking that Sheriff Dobbs and Tater arrived last. In the confusion of the sheriff's interrogation and the paramedics checking her out, Adeline lost track of Gage. By the time the paramedics removed the oxygen mask and released her to Lily and Delaney's care, Gage's truck was gone and so was he.

She drove back to the house with the rest of her family. When she got there, Gretchen fussed over her and drew her a hot bath while Lily brought her a cup of tea. Delaney lay on her bed in shock that Jasper had been the one responsible for everything that had happened on the ranch.

"I just can't believe Jasper would do what he did."

If she hadn't witnessed his craziness with her own eyes, Adeline wouldn't have believed it either. Even after all he'd done, she was still sad about his death. He had been family. She couldn't help wondering how they would break the news to Uncle Jack.

Once Lily, Delaney, and Gretchen left, Adeline wandered out to the balcony to breathe in the fresh air. The sun was setting. Clouds dispersed the bright yellow fireball into deep tangerine tinged with red. She was enjoying the sight when she glanced down and saw Gage emerging from the trees.

He had changed clothes. The blue western shirt fit his broad shoulders perfectly. As did his wrangler jeans. He wore a straw cowboy hat, but took it off as he neared the house. His hair was damp and curled in waves the color of sunshine. He tipped his head back and looked at her. She didn't know how she had ever thought he wasn't a handsome man. He was the handsomest man she had ever seen in her life.

"Hey," he called up.

"Hey," she called down.

He lowered his gaze to the wall as if he was—

"Oh, no," she yelled. "Don't you dare. Come in the back door like a normal person."

He nodded and disappeared out of sight. She raced back inside to check her hair and put on a little lip gloss. She thought about changing out of her robe into a nice dress, but then vetoed the idea. Robes slipped off much easier than dresses.

When more than a few minutes had passed and Gage still wasn't tapping on her door, she started to wonder if her brothers hadn't delayed him. If they had, there was going to be hell to pay. She headed to the door. But when she threw it open, she found Gage pacing in the hallway with hat in hand.

He froze when he saw her, and his face turned red.

"What are you doing?" she asked.

He cleared his throat. "I was just . . . trying to figure out what I was going to say."

She smiled. "How about if you just say what you feel? How about if we both do?" He nodded and stepped inside her room. His gaze immediately went to the bed.

"Maybe we should have this conversation somewhere else."

"Like where?" She closed the door . . . and locked it. "In case you haven't noticed, I have a large family that always seems to be around."

"I noticed. Your brothers gave me the third degree about my intentions before they'd let me come up."

She crossed her arms over her chest, completely aware of how the opening gaped and displayed her cleavage. "And just what are your intentions, Gage Reardon?"

His gaze slipped lower and remained there for a long sizzling moment before it lifted back to her face. "To apologize. I'm sorry, Adeline. I'm sorry for lying to you about why I came here. But mostly I'm sorry for blaming you for something that wasn't your fault."

He took a deep breath and then slowly released it. "From the first time Danny showed me your picture and started telling me stories about you, I had trouble getting you out of my mind. You were this sweet hometown girl who embodied everything I wanted for myself. When Danny told me that you had broken it off with him, I should've been upset for my buddy. Instead, there was this tiny spark of hope that maybe . . . you could be my girl."

He swallowed hard. "So now you know why I felt so guilty after Danny died. The only way I could alleviate that guilt was to turn you into a cold, uncaring princess who tricked men into falling for her and then broke their hearts. But I was wrong, Addie. Completely wrong. You are a sweet hometown girl. Deep now, I always knew it. I might've come here for all the wrong reasons, but I stayed for only one." Tears filled his eyes.

"You. Please forgive me, Adeline. Because I don't think I can live without you."

All her life Adeline had been waiting to feel the kind of intense feelings she felt as she looked into Gage's tear-filled eyes. She had questioned if he was the right man for her. But her heart had always known.

She walked over and took his hands, linking their fingers. "I love you. And I'm not about to let you go that easily. Not when I've finally fallen head over heels. But before we continue, we need to get a few things straight. I'm no princess to be put on a pedestal and admired. Nor am I the sweet hometown girl in a yellow prom dress that you carried around in your wallet. I'm a flesh and blood woman who doesn't want someone worshipping at my feet. I want someone standing by my side, sharing in my hopes and dreams just like I share in his."

His fingers tightened on hers and his gaze grew intense. "I want to be that man. I want to help you achieve all your dreams—whether it's becoming a veterinarian or president of the United States."

She laughed. "I think a vet will do. And one more thing. No more secrets between us. If there's something you haven't told me, you best spit it out now."

"There's nothing else I haven't told you. I'm an ex-Marine whose family owns a big ranch. I love cows and horses . . . and you." He pulled her into his arms and held her close. "I love you, baby. I love you so damn much. I didn't realize how much until Jasper took you. I was scared to death

I wouldn't get to you in time."

She drew back and smiled. "But you did. My warrior saved me."

He shook his head. "No, you saved me. If you hadn't tripped Jasper, we might both be dead. And if you hadn't stopped me from going back into the house, I would sure be."

"Then I guess Hester was right again. I am the hero." She tipped her head. "And I think heroes should get some kind of reward for their bravery, don't you?" She slipped off her robe.

Gage's gaze slid over her naked body and his nostrils flared. But instead of pulling her into his arms, he closed his eyes and groaned. "I can't. I gave my word to Stetson that I wouldn't have sex with you again until we're married."

"Well, we'll just see about—" She cut off when his words sunk in. "Married?"

He pulled a small box from his pocket. "I'd get down on one knee, but you just told me you don't want a man kneeling at your feet." He opened the box to reveal a perfect diamond solitaire. The uncertainty on his face made her heart tighten. "I know it's not very big, but it's special. It's my Nana's ring. She gave it to me a long time ago and has been praying ever since that I'd find the right girl to give it to. You're the only girl I want to wear it. Will you marry me, Adeline?" His gaze swept her body. "Quickly?"

She dove into his arms and covered his face with kisses. "Yes. A thousand times yes." She drew back and held out her hand. "Now give me that beautiful ring." Once he slid it on her finger, she hooked her arms around his neck and gave him a deep, thorough kiss that left him moaning.

"Addie, you're killing me."

"You're killing yourself. Are you going to let my brother boss you around? Or are you going to let me boss you around?"

His eyes widened before a smile spread over his face. "Whatever you say, Boss."

He scooped her up in his arms and carried her to the bed . . . where he made all her wishes come true.

# Chapter Twenty-one

"I LIKE THAT GAL. Adeline reminds me of myself when I was her age."

With difficulty, Gage pulled his gaze away from his bride and turned to his grandmother, who was sitting in a folding chair presiding over the wedding reception like a queen. The string of overhead lights reflected off her silver hair and made her hazel eyes twinkle even more than usual. He had missed those twinkling eyes. While he would love to join his new wife on the dance floor, there would be plenty of time for dancing. In fact, he had the rest of his life to dance with Adeline. Right now, he was content to hang with his granny.

"If she acts like you, then I'm in big trouble," he said with a wink.

Nana swatted his arm. "Mind your manners, young man. You're still not too big to take over my knee."

The thought of his eighty-four-year-old grandmother taking him over his knee made him smile. Of course, he'd been smiling ever since Adeline had agreed to marry him. He'd let her pick the date and had been surprised when she'd chosen one only two weeks later. Although seeing as how they hadn't been careful with birth control, it was probably for the best. The thought of blond, blue-eyed babies had him smiling even bigger.

"You look as happy as a bug in a rug." Nana sighed. "I never thought this day would come. And I'm not talking about you getting married. I'm talking about you finding yourself. When you got back from Iraq, I thought you'd lost yourself for good." She paused and tears filled her aged eyes. "I thought we'd lost you for good."

He put an arm around her and pulled her close. "I did too, Nana. But all your praying must have worked. God gave me exactly what I needed to find myself."

She hugged him tight for a moment before she drew back. "So does that mean you're bringing your new bride back to the ranch to live?"

Gage had done a lot of thinking about that. He loved his family. He loved Sagebrush Ranch. But . . .

His grandmother sighed. "Since you're taking so long to answer, I'm going to assume the answer is no. I guess Adeline doesn't want to leave her family. I can't blame her. They seem like a good bunch."

"They are, but Adeline isn't the reason. She told me that she'd be happy to move."

"Then what's holding you back from coming home?"

Gage looked around at his friends and family.

Adeline had wanted the wedding to be held in the garden with just family and the reception to be held here in the barn with the entire town. Potts was serving smoked brisket and chicken and a live country and western band played on a stage by the corral. A dance floor had been set up in front of the stage. Stetson was leading Lily in a slow two-step and looking thoroughly besotted. Buck danced with Mystic while exchanging jabs with Delaney who was dancing with Wolfe.

Adeline danced with Gage's father. She didn't wear a white wedding gown fit for a princess or a yellow prom dress fit for a hometown girl. Instead, she wore a simple white sundress that showed off her womanly body and her long legs in the sexy red cowboy boots.

She glanced over and saw him watching her. A soft smile lit her face and wiggled its way straight to his heart. Nana was right. Gage had been lost. But now he was found. And he knew who he was and where he wanted to stay.

He smiled back at his bride before he turned to his grandmother. "Sagebrush Ranch will always be my childhood home, Nana. But the Kingman Ranch has become my adult home. It's where I found myself and where I belong . . . at least for now. I like working with horses instead of cattle. And I like being Stetson's right-hand man, instead of my siblings' baby brother. I'm sorry. I know y'all miss me. And I miss you too. But—"

"A man has to find his own place in the world." Nana reached up and patted his cheek. "You always did have your own mind."

He held her hand to his cheek. "Just like someone else I know."

She stared back at him for a long moment, her eyes filled with love before she removed her hand from his cheek and pointed a finger at him. "I'll expect you to come visit every chance you get. Especially when you have babies."

"Yes, ma'am. And I expect you to come visit too. There are plenty of rooms in the Kingman castle."

Nana snorted and shook her head. "A castle. When you first told me about it, I thought you were pullin' my leg. But it does look like it came straight out of a storybook." Her eyes twinkled. "And it looks like you've found your happily-ever-after."

He had. He certainly had.

"Hey, Gage!" Buck hollered. "Come on, bro. It's time to toss the garter."

Gage gave his grandmother one more tight squeeze before he joined Adeline on the dance floor. It looked like she'd had her fair share of the spiked lemonade the Cursed Ladies' Auxiliary Club was serving at the refreshment table. Her blue eyes twinkled like the stars that filled the night sky and her cheeks were the color of the pink roses in the garden. When he knelt in front of her and slipped a hand beneath the hem of her dress, a very naughty smile tipped her lips.

"I like where this is headed," she said in a sultry voice.

After taking his time slipping off the garter, he smoothed down the hem of her dress. "Behave,

Mrs. Reardon." He leaned closer and whispered. "Until later."

One of the cowboys ended up catching the garter. Gage gave him twenty bucks for it. He didn't care what tradition dictated. He didn't want some yahoo having Adeline's garter. He didn't care about the bouquet. Like the rest of the men, he laid bets on what single woman would end up snagging it.

"My bet's on Del," Buck said. "My wildcat sister isn't going to let anyone beat her in a competition."

"I don't know," Wolfe said. "Mystic might have her grandmother's magical forces on her side."

"I'm betting on Lorelei." Stetson put in his five dollars. "That woman has been beating people out for bouquets for years." He glanced at Gage. "Who are you picking, Gage?"

Gage thought for a moment before he made his choice. "My money's on Gretchen. She might be all smiles and southern charm, but I think she's more calculating than anyone realizes."

But when Adeline tossed the bouquet high into the air, Gretchen made no move to catch. In fact, she stepped completely away from the women vying for it. Delaney, on the other hand, elbowed her way through the group of women and jumped like a NBA player going for a rebound. But she only tipped the bouquet and sent it careening into the watching crowd. It looked like it was headed straight for Hester Malone. But then, suddenly, it changed course and landed right at Wolfe's feet.

"Looks like my big brother is gettin' married next!" Buck bellowed, and everyone burst out laughing.

Everyone but Wolfe.

His face darkened into a scowl. "When hell freezes over."

Gage was still laughing when Adeline showed up and took his hand. Without saying a word, she led him through the crowd. He went more than willingly. He would always go wherever his Addie led. But he was curious.

"Where are you taking me?"

"To the stables."

"Hmm? Fixin' to do a little riding, Mrs. Reardon?"

Instead of answering, she pulled him into the darkness of the stables and kissed him. When he was hard and breathless, she drew back and ran a finger along the open collar of his shirt. "As a matter of fact, I am planning on doing a little riding tonight. But first, I wanted to give you your wedding present."

He slid his hands over her butt and pulled her closer. "I'm looking forward to it."

She smiled. "It's not that."

"No?" He inched up her dress. "Are you sure? Because I can't think of a better present than you in my arms completely naked."

Her eyes flared with passion, but before he could get another kiss, she pulled out of his arms. "I'll be more than happy to get naked . . . just not until I give you your gift." She tugged him toward Magnolia's stall.

Now that Glory Boy was no longer at the ranch, it was hard to go near the stall. Glory's new owners had come to get him a few weeks earlier. Watching him leave the ranch had been one of the hardest things Gage had ever had to do. Even now, his eyes got a little misty as they approached the stall.

"What are you doing, Addie?" he asked.

She released his hand and smiled. "Happy Wedding Day, Gage."

He looked at her in confusion before he peeked over the open door of the stall. At first, all he saw was Magnolia Breeze. But then a cute face with big brown eyes peeked under his mama's belly.

"Glory Boy?" he said.

The foal came around his mother and pranced to the open stall door. Gage stroked his velvety head before he turned to Adeline. "How did you get him back?"

She shrugged. "Everyone has a price. And Stetson helped me negotiate the deal. He said he'd made a big mistake selling Glory." She petted Glory's muzzle. "The owners didn't hesitate to take our offer when they found out about the results of the tests you ran on the oat horse treats."

The results had proven the treats had been laced with poison. After the sheriff had searched Jasper's apartment over the bar, they'd found a bottle of the exact same poison. Gage could tell by Adeline's sad expression she was still stunned by her cousin's betrayal.

"I don't understand how he could have done it," she said in a soft voice. "He always loved animals."

Gage pulled her into his arms. "I know, baby. But, sometimes, pain or jealousy or hate can consume you and make you forget who you are. That happened to me in Iraq. I saw so much killing and hate I forgot there was kindness and love in the world too—I forgot there was kindness and love in me. Jasper just forgot who he was."

"I wish I had known how he felt. I wish I could've helped him."

"Hey." He lifted her chin and looked into her tear-filled eyes. "Wasn't it you who told me that I can't save everyone? Jasper chose to keep his pain hidden and not ask for help. If he had, I know you and your entire family would've rallied around him. The Kingmans are the definition of loyalty." He brushed the tears from her eyes. "Thank you for buying back Glory Boy. If any horse is a Kingman horse, it's this foal right here."

She smiled. "You mean a Reardon horse. I bought him for you, Gage. He's yours. He always has been."

There were no words to express the emotion that filled Gage's heart. So he didn't try to use words. Instead, he kissed her. In the kiss, he expressed all his gratefulness. Not just for Glory Boy, but also for waking him after he'd been sleepwalking through life for so long. He knew she didn't want him thinking of her as a princess. But she would always be a princess to him. His princess.

He drew away from the kiss. "I love you, Addie."

She smiled. "I love you too. Now come on."

She took his hand and pulled him out the stable door.

"Where are we going?"

"To my tower." She glanced back at him, her blue eyes twinkling with mischief. "I want to ride my dragon."

## The End

*Turn the page for a special*
SNEAK PEEK
*of the next Kingman Ranch novel.*

## SNEAK PEEK!
# *Charming a Big Bad Texan*

*Coming May 2022!*

---

HOME.

As far as Gretchen Maribel Flaherty was concerned, it was the best word in the dictionary. *The place where one lives permanently, especially as a member of a family or household.*

Gretchen had never had a home. She and her mama had lived in a lot of places. But never permanently. And Mama only claimed her as family when it suited her. Consequently, Gretchen had never felt like she belonged anywhere.

Until now.

If anyone had told her that someday she'd be living in a fairytale castle, she would've laughed herself silly. Logical girls like Gretchen didn't dream about living in beautiful castles. They knew castles were reserved for queens and princesses. Gretchen had never been, nor would she ever be, a queen or a princess. She was just a plain ol' country gal who had gotten unruly red hair and freckles from her daddy and too many teeth and a slow metabolism from her mama.

And yet, she'd somehow stumbled into a fairytale—purely by accident—and was now living the dream. She still wasn't a queen or princess. She was a housekeeper. But she loved her cozy little room behind the kitchen, and she loved working for the five Kingman siblings who ran the Kingman Ranch . . . well, maybe not all five. There was one who had taken a dislike to Gretchen. He was the only one standing in her way of making Kingman Ranch her permanent home.

But she refused to worry about that now. Tonight, she didn't want to think about anything but enjoying her bubble bath.

The tub was huge and surrounded by pretty sand-colored marble tile that reflected the candles Gretchen had lit. The flickering light danced on the shiny chrome fixtures and reflected in the clear bubbles that surrounded her.

She sank deeper in the hot water and sighed with contentment. It just went to show you that, one day, you could be feeling lost and alone and, the next, you could be living in a castle surrounded by bubbles.

The water started to cool, and Gretchen used her toes to turn on the spigots. As she did, her heel accidentally bumped the handheld sprayer and knocked it into the tub. It turned on and a spray of water shot between Gretchen's legs, hitting a spot that had her eyes widening. She grabbed the nozzle. But instead of turning it off, she held it right where it was and closed her eyes.

A fantasy took shape.

*The bathroom door opened and a cowboy stepped in. A broad-shouldered cowboy who wore a Stetson tugged low on his forehead. He moved toward her, his dusty boots clicking on the tile floor as he grew closer and closer. When he reached her, he pulled off his cowboy hat, revealing the thick waves of raven hair.*

Gretchen's eyes opened and she frowned. No, not raven hair. Blond. Ordinary blond hair. She closed her eyes and returned to her fantasy.

*Tossing his hat aside, the ordinary blond cowboy knelt next to the bathtub, his smoky gray eyes—*

Her eyes flashed open again. Not smoky gray eyes. Blue eyes. Plain ol' blue eyes. She closed her eyes and tried to concentrate.

*The ordinary blond cowboy with the plain blue eyes dipped his hand beneath the bubbles and his lips lowered to her mouth as he growled . . .*

"You want me to devour you, darlin'?"

Gretchen was about to say "yes" when someone answered for her.

"Devour me, Wolfe. Please devour me."

Gretchen's eyes flashed opened and she sat up so quickly she sloshed water on the floor. But she didn't worry about the mess she'd made when the growling voice came through the door again.

"You bet, darlin'. Just give me a minute." The doorknob started to turn.

Quickly, Gretchen blew out the candles and ducked under the water. The sprayer was still on. But she couldn't turn it off without it coming out of the faucet and alerting the man who was walking in the door. So she held it under the water with her and prayed she could hold her breath long enough. After what felt like forever, she resurfaced. As soon as she did, she heard.

"What the hell is the matter with you?"

Figuring the jig was up, Gretchen opened her eyes and peeked over the edge of the tub. But Wolfe Kingman wasn't standing there glaring at her. He stood at one of the double sinks with his hands braced on the granite counter. He hadn't turned on the light, but there was enough moonlight coming in the skylight for Gretchen to see him. He wore his standard black t-shirt that looked like it was painted to his hard muscles and faded jeans that hugged his fine butt and long legs.

To say Wolfe was handsome would be like saying the Mona Lisa was a nice painting. His facial features were about as perfect as a man could get without looking too feminine. His cheekbones were high. His lips were wide and full. And his lashes long and dark. With his penetrating smoky-gray eyes, continual five-o'clock stubble, and wealth of wavy black hair, it was no wonder women threw themselves at his boots. The woman in the other room was no doubt waiting to do the same.

So why was Wolfe in here giving himself a pep talk?

"This has never happened to you before and it's not going to happen to you now." He stared at his reflection. "You just need to relax and think about the sexy, hot woman waiting naked for you." He closed his eyes and lowered his hand.

Gretchen's eyes widened as he flicked open the

button of his jeans and lowered the zipper. They widened even more when he slipped his hand inside. The reality that was playing out in front of her was twice as hot as the fantasy she'd just conjured up. She started to adjust the sprayer when Wolfe's hand dropped away and he hung his head between his shoulders.

"Shit."

The door opened, and Wolfe quickly straightened and zipped up his jeans as the light came on and a beautiful blond stepped in as naked as the day she was born. Wolfe hadn't lied. The woman was the definition of hot and sexy. She had full breasts that seemed to defy gravity and a flat stomach that probably had never digested a slice of chocolate cake in its life.

The woman walked over and gave Wolfe a scorching kiss that caused Gretchen's face to burn. As she kissed him, she slid her hand over his fly. She drew away and smiled seductively.

"It feels like you could use a little warming up." She lowered to her knees.

Gretchen released a tiny gasp, then quickly pressed her lips closed. But it was too late. Both the woman and Wolfe turned to the bathtub. The woman jumped to her feet and pointed a finger at Gretchen.

"Who the hell are you?" The woman didn't let her answer before she turned back to Wolfe. "So this is why you acted so strange when I wanted to come up to your room. You had another woman waiting for you."

"Oh," Gretchen said. "I'm not one of Mr.

Kingman's—"

Wolfe cut her off. "Now, Sue Ann, you know I never double dip. I didn't know she'd be here. Just like I didn't know you'd follow me home from town."

The explanation and Wolfe's charming smile seemed to take all the anger right out of Sue Ann. She cuddled close to his naked chest. "That's alright, baby." She sent Gretchen a forced smile. "I'll just wait in the other room while you get rid of her."

Gretchen figured Wolfe would take Sue Ann up on the offer, but instead he completely surprised her. "Now, darlin'. That wouldn't be fair. Not when she was here first."

Sue Ann's eyes widened. "Are you saying you choose that red-headed cow over me?"

Gretchen stiffened. "Red-headed cow? Now wait one—"

Wolfe held up his hands. "Ladies, ladies, there's no need to fight. What do you say we call it a draw and I don't sleep with either one of you tonight?"

"A draw?" Sue Ann released a loud, angry huff before she stormed out of the bathroom, slamming the door behind her. When she was gone, Wolfe slowly turned to Gretchen. The charming smile was gone, replaced with the same annoyed, confused look he always gave her—like she was a cold sore that had popped up out of nowhere and he couldn't figure out how to get rid of.

Wolfe was the only Kingman who didn't like her. In fact, he'd made no bones about wanting her fired. And she couldn't blame him. The more she tried to make him like her, the more klutzy she became.

She had spilled coffee, sweet tea, soup, and a variety of other liquids on him. She'd walked in on him when he was showering, lost his socks in the laundry, vacuumed up his Airpods ... and even set fire to his bed. None of it had been intentional. But he didn't seem to believe that. If it were up to him, Gretchen would've been fired already.

She didn't want to get fired.

The Kingman Ranch was her home.

Which is why she couldn't give up trying to get Wolfe to like her.

"I am so sorry, sir," she said as she sunk lower in the bubbles that seem to be popping as she spoke. "I didn't mean to mess up your ... evening. You see, the faucet in my bathtub sprung a leak. Your sister Adeline said I could use one of the bathrooms upstairs until the plumber can get here on Monday to fix mine. And since you were in Amarillo lookin' at horses and your bathroom had this big ol' tub that wasn't being used, I thought you wouldn't mind if—"

He cut her off. "But I do mind, Miss Flaherty. I mind a lot. I have repeatedly asked you to stay out of my room and repeatedly you have ignored me."

"But I'm the housekeeper, Mr. Kingman. I have to supervise the maids and make sure your room is being cleaned properly. It's my job."

"And what does walking in while I'm showering have to do with making sure my room is clean?"

Her face flushed at the memory of seeing his naked body all soaped up. "I was just putting fresh towels in your bathroom. The door wasn't locked. Although there must be something wrong with that latch because I locked it tonight and you walked right in." She smiled brightly. "So I guess that makes us even."

He spoke through gritted teeth. "Not even close. I want you to stay away from me. I don't want you in my room. I don't want you in my bathroom. And I don't want you in my tub. Do I make myself clear?"

"Yes, sir!" She went to do a little salute, but she forgot about the spray nozzle in her hand. As soon as it was out of the water, spray shot through the air . . . and hit Wolfe right in the face.

"Oh, no!" Gretchen gasped as she tried to find the shut off button. When she couldn't, she sat up and turned off the spigots.

But it was too late.

By the time she looked back, Wolfe was drenched from his thick raven hair to his lizard-skin boots. His jaw worked back and forth like he was a cow chewing on a nasty piece of cud. Then his gaze lowered, and his jaw stopped moving and his lips parted on a surprised puff of air.

When Gretchen glanced down, she understood why. Her boobs were no longer covered in bubbles. They hung there like two huge water balloons. She released a little squeal before she crossed her arms over her chest and slid back down in the water.

For a long, embarrassing moment, Wolfe stood there staring at the water with its thin later of bubbles before he turned on a boot hell and walked out, slamming the door behind him.

Once he was gone, Gretchen quickly got out of the tub and dried off with a towel. "You've done it now, Gretchen Maribel Flaherty. If this doesn't get you fired, nothing will." She pulled on her chenille robe and hurried out of the bathroom, hoping to apologize . . . and discovered a shirtless Wolfe stripping off his wet jeans.

Just like when she'd walked in on him taking a shower, she became paralyzed by his masculine beauty. By the artfully arranged muscles. The perfect sprinkling of dark hair. And the sexy snarling wolf tattoo. Unable to do anything else, she stood there ogling him like a Magic Mike strip show. If she'd had any dollars, it would've been raining money.

Unfortunately, he didn't appreciate her appreciation. He jerked his jeans back up and pointed a finger at the door. "Out! Now!"

Preorder on Amazon now!
*https://tinyurl.com/yck537t2*

# Other Titles by Katie Lane

Be sure to check out all of Katie Lane's novels!
*www.katielanebooks.com*

### Kingman Ranch Series
*Charming a Texas Beast*
*Charming a Knight in Cowboy Boots*
*Charming a Big Bad Texan (May 2022)*

### Bad Boy Ranch Series:
*Taming a Texas Bad Boy*
*Taming a Texas Rebel*
*Taming a Texas Charmer*
*Taming a Texas Heartbreaker*
*Taming a Texas Devil*
*Taming a Texas Rascal*
*Taming a Texas Tease*
*Taming a Texas Christmas Cowboy*

### Brides of Bliss Texas Series:
*Spring Texas Bride*
*Summer Texas Bride*
*Autumn Texas Bride*
*Christmas Texas Bride*

### Tender Heart Texas Series:
*Falling for Tender Heart*
*Falling Head Over Boots*

*Falling for a Texas Hellion*
*Falling for a Cowboy's Smile*
*Falling for a Christmas Cowboy*

## Deep in the Heart of Texas Series:
*Going Cowboy Crazy*
*Make Mine a Bad Boy*
*Catch Me a Cowboy*
*Trouble in Texas*
*Flirting with Texas*
*A Match Made in Texas*
*The Last Cowboy in Texas*
*My Big Fat Texas Wedding*

## Overnight Billionaires Series:
*A Billionaire Between the Sheets*
*A Billionaire After Dark*
*Waking up with a Billionaire*

## Hunk for the Holidays Series:
*Hunk for the Holidays*
*Ring in the Holidays*
*Unwrapped*

# About the Author

KATIE LANE IS a firm believer that love conquers all and laughter is the best medicine. Which is why you'll find plenty of humor and happily-ever-afters in her contemporary and western contemporary romance novels. A USA Today Bestselling Author, she has written numerous series, including *Deep in the Heart of Texas, Hunk for the Holidays, Overnight Billionaires, Tender Heart Texas, The Brides of Bliss Texas, Bad Boy Ranch,* and *Kingman Ranch*. Katie lives in Albuquerque, New Mexico, and when she's not writing, she enjoys reading, eating chocolate (dark, please), and snuggling with her high school sweetheart and Cairn Terrier, Roo.

For more on her writing life or just to chat, check out Katie here:
Facebook *www.facebook.com/katielaneauthor*
Instagram *www.instagram.com/katielanebooks*

And for information on upcoming releases and great giveaways, be sure to sign up for her mailing list at *www.katielanebooks.com*!

Printed in Great Britain
by Amazon